THE PROMISE OF
CHRISTMAS PAST

THE PROMISE OF CHRISTMAS PAST

A MACKINAC ISLAND NOVELLA

LINDA HUGHES

For Mackinac Island lovers everywhere ~
Those who live and work there, those who visit,
and those who dream of being there.

1

MACKINAC ISLAND, DECEMBER 21, 1822

Crusty snow crunched underfoot as Gichi shuffled from side to side in an attempt to fend off the blistering cold. Thankfully her fur wrap, wool cap and mittens, and fur-lined moccasins kept out most of the chill. At least there was no cutting wind and the sun shone, so it wasn't dark and dreary as winter days had wont to be.

Still, even in all its haunting beauty, it was the winter solstice, what her mother and Madame La Framboise called solstice d'hiver when they slipped into French, the shortest day of the year. And it was frightfully cold.

That hadn't thwarted the thirty people who watched with curious wonder as four men toiled to put up a felled blue spruce tree in the middle of the main street in their small settlement on Mackinac Island. Mr. Schmidt, a German fur trader, had suggested it, saying it had become tradition in his homeland at Christmastime in honor of their Lord Jesus's birth. But no one else on the island had heard of such a tradition regarding that holy day.

Mr. McIntyre, younger and more agile, hollered amicably to Mr. Schmidt. "Throw me the hammer, Günter, and I'll pound in the final nail." The German tossed his hammer to the Irishman, who caught it nimbly, and Mr. McIntyre worked at finishing the job of securing the boards they'd nailed together at the trunk of the tree to make it stand up.

Gichi didn't understand why they'd cut down the magnificent tree in the first place only to make it stand up again. She'd heard the story of the nativity many times from the books of Luke and Matthew in the *Bible*, and she couldn't figure out how this tree had anything to do with it. There had been Mary and Joseph, angels, a manger, animals, shepherds, the Star of Bethlehem, Magi, and Baby Jesus. No blue spruce tree.

But even though she knew she was smart for her seven years of walking the earth, she also knew she didn't know everything and needed to defer – most of the time anyway – to the adults. That was hard to do sometimes because the adults – Americans, French Canadians, Brits, the visiting parish priest, the new protestant preacher, her godmother Madame La Framboise, her Odawa mother, their clan's chief, chiefs from other clans, and more – didn't always agree. But Gichi did her best to put it all together.

There must be some hidden symbol in this ritual of putting up a Christmas tree that she didn't yet understand. Consequently, she'd need to wait for the mysterious and magical meaning to unfold.

However, at the moment the tree wasn't as interesting as Mr. McIntyre, the Irish fisherman who was from a faraway place called Eire. There were a few other Irishmen on the island, but Gichi didn't know them. Mr. McIntyre was her friend. The stories he gifted her with about his homeland drew pictures in her head of gloriously green rolling hills by a sea with even bigger waves than her lakes Huron and Michigan. The grownups called him Niall, but naturally, being a mere girl, she couldn't address him with such familiarity.

Not that she ever addressed anyone in any way. Having no voice and not speaking made life easier in many ways. For one, she didn't have to worry about what to call anybody.

Once she overheard her mother explain her silence to a visitor. "She cried and babbled like all babies and talked in full sentences by the time she was two. But when her father died of influenza when she was three, she ceased talking. No one has been able to get a word out of her since. Dr. Beaumont, the post surgeon, speculates she had a light case of influenza, too, that affected her vocal cords. But I'm not so sure."

Gichi wasn't sure either.

She watched Mr. McIntyre as he squatted to work at the base of the tree. He was a handsome man. She knew that because she heard the women say it all the time when he wasn't around. Gichi didn't know anything about that, but she did know she loved his stories and the way he was so kind to her. Most adults avoided her because she didn't talk, but he didn't seem to mind that at all. Besides, he talked enough for both of them. He'd been on the island for six months and she found herself wishing he was her father. Her real one died when she was so little, she hardly remembered him except for the feeling of being safe in his arms and his smell, fur and hides and sweat, that meant he was home from working and her world was complete. She felt the same thing from Mr. McIntyre, although he often smelled like fish. If she did have another father, she wanted it to be him.

A horse-drawn sleigh suddenly appeared as it rounded a corner from a side road, and Gichi could see that Mr. Wright and his daughter, one Miss Rebecca Wright, were on an outing with their driver at the reins. They were Americans. He was a boss man for Mr. Astor's American Fur Company. Normally, except for the soldiers stationed at the fort and a few of the fur company's warehouse workers, Americans wouldn't be on the island in the wintertime because business with the Indians and fur traders went on in the spring and summer. Most Americans, especially the fancy ones, left before rough weather hit.

But Mr. Wright had broken his leg and had to stay while it healed. He and his daughter were bundled up in fur blankets, but his stiff leg in its thick bandages could still be made out underneath all the covers.

The sleigh slowed to a crawl to take the turn, barely slipping past the Christmas tree. The people standing on that side to watch the raising of the tree had to move out of the way. Gichi noticed that no one in the sleigh – not Mr. Wright, his daughter, or the driver – acknowledged the accommodation. She had been taught to always nod in appreciation when someone did something nice for her. She thought these particular Americans were not very nice.

Many others thought so, too. Miss Wright had been the favorite of gossips ever since arriving last summer. "Hoity-toity" her mother called the young woman who wore shiny dresses with billowing skirts. Gichi didn't understand American women's clothes. They looked mighty uncomfortable. She thought herself lucky to have been born a Métis with Odawa and French-Canadian blood so she didn't have to contend with such foolishness as petticoats and flimsy slipper-shoes. Even Madame La Framboise, a Métis widow with French ladylike manners and American-like business success in the fur trade, preferred wearing her Odawa clothes. In fact, Gichi had overheard many a businessman who visited the house comment on how fetching she looked in her colorful native attire.

Miss Wright's dress on this day wasn't visible under the pile of fur blankets, but the hood of a fox-lined, blue velvet cape escaped to cover her head. Blond curls poked out on the sides of her dainty face and her blue eyes glistened in the freezing cold, reminding Gichi of blue ice.

All heads turned to look at the young woman.

Mr. McIntyre stood up and fumbled with the hammer he held in one hand, clumsily caught it in his other hand, and smiled broadly at Miss Wright. She looked at him blankly, her frozen features unmoved. The sleigh completed the corner and moved on. The crowd stared at its behind as if the king and queen had passed by.

Mr. Schmidt broke the spell by clapping his gloved hands and pointing at the tree, which finally stood on its own. He gestured for Mr. McIntyre to speak.

"Ladies and gents, lasses and lads, we bring you Mackinac Island's first Christmas tree!" he shouted joyously, his Irish brogue more prominent than usual in his excitement as he circled the tree with outstretched arms. "And remember, come back tomorrow to see

Mr. Schmidt decorate it with the tin stars he's made. Correct, Mr. Schmidt?"

"Ya-a-ah, fer su-u-ure," the stout man agreed, his accent so thick it seemed he'd hardly left that placed called Germany that was so far away.

The small crowd clapped, gloves and mittens muting the sound, and people started to disperse. It was then that Mr. McIntyre noticed Gichi.

"And there she be! Me bonnie colleen." He came over and she threw him a gap-toothed grin, having lost an incisor the day before. He'd given her a half penny when he'd seen the hole in her teeth. Now he patted her shoulder and said, "What do you say we get out of this wretched cold? Do you think your ma might make us a wee bit of steaming hot tea?"

She nodded enthusiastically, and they trod through the snow toward Madame La Framboise's residence on the edge of town. The wood-slat house with the gabled roof was Gichi's permanent home with her mother who worked there and Mr. McIntyre's temporary home while he rented one of the guest rooms. He had big plans to make an American fortune by building a fishing business.

"Don't you know, Gichi colleen," he said as they walked past the fort that loomed above them up on the bluff, "that my family back home in Galway celebrates Christmas with a fine meal, to be sure. Me ma makes lamb stew and me pa catches us a fine salmon. There's soda bread, different from the bread you have here. And steamed cabbage. Do you like steamed cabbage, me love?"

She shrugged. She didn't know.

"Ah, well, you would if you had some of me ma's. And then me granny makes us a fine plum pudding for dessert, if we can get us some plums. All of this after mass, of course. We dinna eat till we've celebrated our Lord Jesus's birth."

She nodded. It was the same here. Madame La Framboise saw to it that they worshipped first then had a wonderful meal on Christmas Day. Madame was so devout she'd donated land next to her house so

Saint Anne's Catholic Church could be moved there from the center of town.

Gichi suddenly had an urge to tell Mr. McIntyre the amazing story about how the log church had been moved from the mainland to the island, hauled over frozen Lake Huron one winter long ago. But, of course, she couldn't tell him. He'd probably heard it from someone else anyway, it was such an often-told tale.

Mr. McIntyre chatted the whole way home, his Irish brogue charming Gichi all the way, and when they got there her mother did indeed invite them into the kitchen where they sat by the fire and drank steaming hot tea. Gichi felt warm from the fire and the tea and, most of all, from being near her friend.

She feared, however, that he was about to be hurt. She'd overheard her mother and Amelia, the Chippewa woman who also worked in the kitchen, talk about it.

Mother had said, "The poor lad. His heart is about to be broken."

"Oui," Amelia replied, "as sure as that lake out there is about to freeze over for the winter."

At first Gichi panicked, thinking that meant the heart in his chest would burst apart for some wicked reason like a rival's curse. After more eavesdropping, however, she figured out Mother meant his feelings were going to be hurt.

But Gichi could see that for herself. Today the woman hadn't so much as nodded at him when he'd graced her with his brilliant smile.

Everyone on the island knew that Niall McIntyre was madly in love. Yes, the Irish fisherman was in love with Miss Rebecca Wright, the daughter of the wealthy American. And everyone but he could see that Miss Rebecca Wright was not in love with him.

Gichi had even overheard Madame say, "Niall is naïve regarding the potency of a disingenuous woman's wiles. His handsomeness has made him her victim, and in his inexperience, he doesn't realize it. She teases him and toys with him for her own entertainment and self-aggrandizement. But love? I fear not."

Even though Gichi hadn't understood what each of those words meant, she got the gist. She knew a jumble of languages – English,

French, Odawa dialects like Ojibwe and Potawatomi, and a smattering of others she heard from foreigners who came to the island – but she didn't always comprehend each word and sometimes had to mull them over to figure out what they meant in the whole of it. What Madame had said meant that Mr. McIntyre was in love and Miss Wright was not.

Even though her mother, other workers, and Madame knew Gichi was smart and understood much of their gossip, they didn't hesitate to speak freely around her. She supposed that was because she didn't talk, consequently they knew she'd never repeat what they said. It gave her a secret inside belonging to the adult world, as if she'd passed a rite of passage vision quest. She knew most children didn't get to do that, and she took the honor seriously.

She drank her tea while watching her friend Mr. McIntyre of the soon-to-be-broken heart jovially regale her mother with a lively tale about putting up the Christmas tree. The way he told a story made Gichi long to tell stories, too.

If only she could speak, she would plead, "Mr. McIntyre, beware of Miss Rebecca Wright! She has wiles that will break your heart!" But, of course, she did not say a word. She set down her teacup and shoved her long black hair behind her ears, as was her habit. She picked up her cup again, and worry showed itself as her hand trembled ever so slightly while she finished her tea.

2

WEST BRANCH, MICHIGAN, JUNE 21, 2022

W
anda's hands trembled as she removed the top from the dilapidated cardboard box and set it aside.

"You're shaking, Mrs. Woods. Are you okay?"

Wanda cringed at the name but wasn't about to tell this stranger she wasn't missus anything anymore. People had known her as Mrs. Woods for twenty-five years whenever she'd come to this town to visit her grandparents, and somehow this young woman knew that. Wanda supposed it was her own fault because she hadn't introduced herself by any name. But now Ms. Roberts, her maiden name, would do just fine.

She didn't know the docent's name and didn't care. She had other things on her mind.

She cast the stinging reminder of her recent divorce-from-the-depths-of-hell aside, scraped her fingers through the sides of her shoulder-length auburn hair to stick it out of the way behind her ears, and peered into the musty container. Ignoring the young woman's faux pas, she finally answered the question. "Yeah. I'm okay. It's so unbelievable that you found this."

"I can't believe it either. I'm really glad you came along to get it. I haven't even looked inside yet. I only saw the name on the top. You say you're researching your family history? Have you discovered much yet that you didn't know?"

Distracted by the box, Wanda suddenly felt bitchy for being curt with the young woman. Of course, she always felt guilty about everything anyway, something she'd been working on since the Big D. Still, she realized it would be appropriate to be more appreciative of the museum worker's help.

"No, not much about this side of my family. I've use ancestry.com, but my ancestry on my mother's side is a great big mystery. Of course, that drives me crazy. Even though I'm only an armchair historian, I feel compelled to fill in the gaps as best I can."

"I'm so glad I could help. If I hadn't been looking for Mr. Wiesenbaker's dead grandmother's recipe box so he could make her red velvet pound cake, I never would've come back here into this dark corner."

"Did you find it?" Wanda's friend Gale came up behind them. Petite Gale claimed to stand five feet tall, but Wanda knew she stretched the truth. Seeing that both Wanda and the docent stood half a foot taller, they slid over so Gale could also see into the mysterious box.

The question confused Wanda. "We didn't know what we'd find."

"No, the red velvet pound cake recipe." Gale's gentle Southern accent made it sound even more yummy than it undoubtedly was.

"Oh, yeah, we found it." The docent nodded with satisfaction.

"Butter cream frosting?" Gale wanted to know.

Gale's delivery was so sweet Wanda could almost taste that icing. Gale was a great cook, with traditional southern cooking her specialty.

"Yeah," the docent told Gale. "Butter cream. He's gonna bring me a great big piece when he makes it."

"Aren't you a lucky girl. Now, what have we got here, my friend?"

Wanda almost missed the question, her rapt attention drawn to the contents as she peered inside the box, her eyes wide with wonder.

She held her hands up as if to dig in but hesitated, afraid to touch anything.

"I think I've opened a treasure trove of family history. Gale, I'm glad you and Dawn are here to help me go through it."

On cue, Dawn's footfall could be heard on the wooden steps leading up to them in the attic. She'd been taking photos of the elegant 1920s wedding dress displayed in the main bedroom on the second floor. The nameless docent had given them a tour of the house, now a museum, and the women had been enchanted by the satin gown with its puffy sleeves, braided tie belt, and long train. Having been in the fashion consulting business for years, classy clothing always caught Dawn's practiced eye.

"Did y'all find a million dollars of the family's illegal hush money?" Dawn jibed when she got to the top of the stairs, her southern accent more pronounced than Gale's.

"I wish," Wanda murmured as she finally reached in and fingered a stack of delicate papers, yellowed with age, that sat neatly piled at the top of the box's contents.

Dawn joined in as the four of them marveled at the find. They stood in the attic of the grand Victorian-era house that served as the Ogemaw County Museum in Wanda's grandparents' hometown, West Branch, Michigan. The three friends had stopped by only twenty minutes earlier, and after a quick tour of the house Wanda had off-handedly asked the docent if they had anything from her maternal grandparents, the Steupenhausens. She'd already found copies of a couple of things in the county courthouse archives but hadn't expected to find anything here. So she was stunned to be led to this box that had "Steupenhausen" written in large, faded cursive across the top.

"We have so much stuff, as you can see," the docent noted while swishing a hand around to indicate more boxes and furniture and toys and clutter that filled the vast space with its exposed, rough-hewn, wooden beams overhead and beveled glass windows on either end, "that we haven't gotten to everything yet."

Carefully, as if they might disintegrate in her hands, Wanda took the papers out of the box and looked through them. "A copy of the deed to their house on South 4th Street, like the one I found at the courthouse. That's the house they lived in their entire married lives, where my mom grew up. She went to nursing school in Detroit and met my dad there. He worked at the Ford plant, so I grew up in Dearborn, near Detroit," she explained to the docent, referring to the city that was a couple of hours south of West Branch.

She didn't need to explain to Gale and Dawn because the three of them had heard each other's life stories repeatedly over the past seventeen years. They'd known each other for so long they claimed they had to remain friends because they knew too much. They had to be nice to each other forevermore to ensure secrecy.

They might seem an unlikely trio, but they'd bonded the moment of their happenstance meeting at a flea market. They'd each been looking for furniture to refinish and ended up helping one another, then going to lunch and laughing so hard they decided to do it again the next day. That sealed the deal.

Forty-five-year-old Wanda was strikingly pretty but seldom thought so. Her hair perfectly framed her square-jawed face. She preferred casual clothes, on this day wearing shorts and a tee shirt. Her svelte yet athletic body carried casual well.

Fifty-year-old Gale's curly salt-and-pepper hair accentuated her delicate heart-shaped face. In jeans and a cute top her body could have been twenty-five again. Although a successful real estate agent, she was the queen of thrift shopping but always looked chic no matter the source.

Thirty-five-year-old Dawn had a fashion consulting business so, naturally, was the most stylish. On this day she wore a bright purple designer summer dress that Wanda figured would look like an eggplant if she wore it. But with that dress on her curvy figure, with her long, blunt-cut, prematurely white hair Dawn looked stunning, as usual.

When Wanda decided she wanted to seek out her ancestors, her two best friends readily agreed to join in, saying they needed a vacation, anyway. Therefore, they'd flown from their hometown of Atlanta, Georgia, to Detroit, Michigan, and rented a car to drive north and dig into this branch of Wanda's elusive family tree.

"My parents brought me up here from Detroit to visit Gramma and Grampa all the time," Wanda told the docent as she shuffled through the crinkly old papers. "I loved coming here."

"But I take it you moved south?"

"Yes. After college I moved to Atlanta to be a flight attendant. It was a big move, a big adventure. I've lived there ever since."

She skipped the part about meeting an accountant who also worked for the airline, marrying him, and holding his hand for twenty-five years while he worked his way up to become a muckety-muck executive with the company. She'd quit the job she loved to support him, at his insistence, and to raise their two children who she also loved.

But now the children were grown and gone, and the big-wig who'd turned into a low-life was gone, too, although she doubted he'd ever grown in any way that mattered.

The docent opened her mouth but snapped it shut, apparently realizing that asking any more personal questions, especially about Wanda's marital status, might be rude. After all, the woman hadn't offered any more information.

Wanda turned her attention back to the papers she held in her hand. She put the deed at the bottom of the short stack and looked at the next one. "Here's their marriage certificate."

"Wow, look at the handwriting," Gale noted. "It's so beautiful."

Dawn shook her head in regret. "We sure don't do that anymore."

"No, we don't," Wanda agreed. She held the papers in one hand and lovingly ran the forefinger of her other hand over the document. "They were married for seventy years, until her death. He died a few months later. Everybody said it was a broken heart. We don't see that anymore, either."

Each of her friends, one on either side, patted her back, letting her know they had her back as she referenced her own failed marriage. Both women had loving, supportive, good husbands. And both women despised Wanda's ex, who exhibited none of those traits.

Wanda perused the next document, a receipt for a 1959 Bel Aire. "I remember this car. It was aqua blue and white. Gramps kept it in pristine condition. They bought it new ..."

"Look!" the docent interrupted as she excitedly pointed into the box.

The others looked to see an old, weathered, leather Bible, black with crackled gold lettering on the front and a shadow of gold on the edges of the pages. It looked like it'd been through the Battle of Jericho.

"A family Bible," the docent offered, "might have names and dates recorded, like they used to do."

Wanda looked at her, blinked, and looked back at the book. "I've found a bit online about my grandparents, but nothing before that in my mother's line. My mom insists her mother, my grandmother, never talked about her family, so Mom can't help me. Even though we used to visit them all the time when I was a kid, it never occurred to me then to ask any questions. Questions never crossed my mind until Gramma was gone and it was too late."

"I hear people say that a lot," the docent said. "This might answer some of your questions."

"Honey, open it up." Dawn reached toward it herself then snatched back her hand.

Wanda barely heard her, so intent was her focus on the book that had the potential to change her family, her life, as she knew it. She laid the papers aside on a nearby table, stretched her fingers in anticipation, and lifted the Bible out of the box. After gently blowing on it to dust off the cover, she opened it.

After a few front pages, there it was. "Holy moly, here it is, births, marriages, and deaths on my mother's side of the family going back ..." she counted using a finger "... five generations. How amazing." She whispered her last words in wonder.

"It's yours; you can take it," the docent told her. "It only came here with a bunch of other abandoned stuff from lockboxes that were in the bank that closed twenty years ago. Whoever took care of your grandparents' estate must not have known about it."

Wanda had a hard time processing what the docent said. Instead, her mind swirled and her eyes misted as she tried to take in all those names handwritten on the page in various styles of cursive. The names were as foreign to her as if she read a novel and the dates were from so unimaginably long ago they may as well have been buried ancient history. "Yes. Yes. Thank you. It'll take me a while to go through all this."

"Wait. There's one more thing in the box." Gale stood on her tiptoes to point it out.

The docent reached in and brought out a small, red velvet box, the kind used for a piece of jewelry. It had become so mottled with age it looked like a kitten or a mouse had gnawed it.

With her hands quivering again, Wanda gently placed the Bible back in the cardboard box, took the small jewelry box, and opened the attached top. She marveled at what lay before her. A tarnished locket on a thin chain lay ensconced in tattered red silk. She hesitated. It felt almost as if she were a voyeur stumbling upon a lovers' secret from long ago, a sacred promise meant to be kept private for all eternity.

Eternity be damned, she snatched it up and held it so everyone could see.

"It's beautiful!" Gale exclaimed. "Rather crude looking, but beautiful all the same."

"It looks pre-Victorian," Dawn stated authoritatively. "That flower design on the front isn't quite as fancy as Victorian. It's really, really old. I think it's brass. That's what they used when they couldn't afford silver or gold."

Wanda drew the locket closer to inspect the design. "It looks handmade, probably by a jeweler. Nobody else would've been able to do it."

"Is there anything on the back?" the docent asked.

Wanda turned it over. "Yes, there's something here, but I can't see it well enough to tell what it says. It's so tiny and it's all scratchy. Let me get closer to the light."

She went over to the window where afternoon light streamed in, bright on this clear summer day. The others followed like a brood of waddling ducklings, no one wanting to be left out. Wanda found a good angle to catch the light. "I still can't read it. I need something to try to wipe away some of the tarnish."

"Here." The docent scurried across the room and came back with a rag that looked like it'd been used for cleaning. She handed it to Wanda.

Wanda held the locket in the palm of one hand and used the cotton cloth to rub as hard as possible with the other. "It says 'Christmas ...'" she rubbed some more "... 18-something.'" She squinted. "'1822'!"

Gale let out a low gasp. "1822. Imagine that. Two hundred years ago."

"That's some old piece of history right there," Dawn drawled.

"Wow. Just think," the docent added, "this was up here and we didn't know it. It's a real treasure."

Wanda turned the locket over and looked at the front more closely. Running her thumb along the side, she found what she'd suspected would be there and clicked a minuscule button. The top popped open. "Oh, there's no rendering. I know they didn't have photography yet in 1822, but I'd hoped for a sketch of somebody." Her tone belied her disappointment. "But look! There's more engraving on both sides." She brightened as she read, "This side says, 'To Gigi, Love ...' Damn, I can't read who it's from. But wait." She used the cloth for more rubbing. "It isn't Gigi. It's ... Gichi. G-I-C-H-I. But I still can't tell who it's from."

The four women stared in silence, no one knowing what to say.

Eventually, the docent came up with a possibility. "Gichi, like Gitche Gumee. You know, the Henry Wadsworth Longfellow poem *The Song of Hiawatha*. 'By the shores of Gitche Gumee, by the shining Big-Sea-Water ....'"

Gale and Dawn stared at her, lost.

"They're from the South," Wanda observed. "They didn't learn that poem like we did up north."

"Nope. Never heard of it." Dawn shrugged.

"It sounds lovely though," Gale politely reckoned.

"Every school-kid in Michigan learns that poem – or used to. I did," the young docent said. "It's a Native American tale that's very long but very beautiful. I'm sure you can find it online. Gichi does sound like a native name and seeing that the locket was given to this Gichi, that must be a woman. A locket wouldn't have been given to a man."

"She apparently meant something to my family or this wouldn't have been kept for so long. The names in the Bible start in 1829, and I didn't see anything like Gichi. But here it is, and I'm determined to find out who she was and who gave it to her."

"What's the other side say?" Gale asked.

"Let's see ... it says, 'Mackinac Island'."

"Mackinac Island?" Dawn queried. "Isn't that the island you told us about?"

"Yeah," Gale recalled. "The one with no cars. Horses and bikes and walking."

"Yes," Wanda assured them. "My parents used to take me there every summer when I was a kid. I loved it. But I had no idea it'd be connected to my ancestry."

"We have to go there," Gale said.

"Yes, we must." Dawn nodded adamantly.

"I'd love to go back anyway, and this makes it even more interesting." Wanda placed the necklace back in its jewelry box, set that box in the larger one with the Bible, replaced the papers, put the top back on, and picked up the box.

"Thank you, ah, I'm sorry I didn't catch your name."

The docent smiled. "That's okay. I'm Missy but I go back to college next month. If you need anything else from here, Sally is the main contact."

"Thank you, Missy. I truly appreciate your help. This means a lot to me."

The three friends left in a hurry to start the two-and-a-half-hour drive to the ferry that would take them to Mackinac Island. Wanda was on the hunt for someone named Gichi and an unnamed person who'd given her a locket, someones who may have made Wanda's very existence possible. There was no stopping her now in her quest to unearth the truth about the dead people who made her.

3

MACKINAC ISLAND, DECEMBER 21, 1822

"I suppose you'll be a wonderful mother yourself someday, my child. You'll provide your little island here with lots of Métis children to carry on your heritage."

Gichi squinted in quandary at the American fort commander who sat at the head of Madame's dinner table. Gichi didn't think about "someday" being anything. She liked being a girl. Fortunately, everyone knew she didn't talk, so she didn't have to respond.

Her friend Mr. McIntyre sat across from her and winked. She grinned in return and relaxed.

"I hear that the new protestant preacher who came to visit wants to open a school for Métis and Indian children on the island." The commander addressed Madame La Framboise. Gichi was relieved he'd turned his attention away from her. "What is your opinion of that, Madame? The informal lessons you provide here at your house would then dissolve, I presume?"

Madame politely put down her fork and addressed the officer. The roasted venison and potatoes Mother had made along with beans, dried berries, and buttered buns made an excellent meal. "Yes, most likely. I support Reverend Ferry's efforts. A real school with a school building will be a blessing for our children." She picked up her fork, started to take another bite, but paused. "I'm not worried about our children losing their Catholic faith, in case you're wondering about that, sir, but are too polite to ask. I cannot imagine our children ever losing their Catholic sensibilities. I'll see to it that they don't." Finally, she resumed her meal.

Unfortunately for Gichi, the formidable man insisted on turning his attention back to her. "Gichi, are you happy about the prospect of such a school? I suppose a child like you could still learn something there."

Oh, oh. Gichi watched Mother, Amelia, Mr. McIntyre, and Madame bristle. She could see it happen around the table as one person's back after another stiffened. This might get interesting. They always spoke up for her.

Once, she'd overheard a visitor ask Madame about the "deaf and dumb Indian girl." Madame's voice had become more forceful than usual. "I can assure you, sir, that Gichi St. Croix is more intelligent than ten of us put together. She is neither deaf nor dumb. She simply chooses not to speak, which may be the most intelligent thing any of us could ever do."

The man shut up.

On this night, it was Mr. McIntyre who was the first to interject on her behalf. "Aye, we do hope Gichi enjoys the new school, if it comes to pass."

That was news to her. She'd refused to attend the lessons Madame held right in this house for Métis and Indian children. She had no intention of attending a school, either, with some preacher stranger.

"In the meantime," Mr. McIntyre said, still addressing the commander, "she takes advantage of all there is to learn outdoors. She knows every inch of this island, every animal, stone structure, hill, cave, forest, and plant. She rescues injured animals and nurses them back to life. She finds stray kittens and gives them a home. She even found a grown man once who lost his way in a winter storm on the other side of the island. Aye, all these manly trappers on the island and she's the best tracker of the lot," He'd lain his hand out flat on the table, pointed in her direction, as if reaching out to comfort her. "Should one of your soldiers ever get lost, rest assured Gichi will find him for you."

That got a chuckle out of the commander and the subject was dropped. After that, Madame, the commander, and Mr. McIntyre chatted about boring people in Washington D.C., a place impossibly far away that Gichi had no interest in. The rest of them remained quiet, paying attention to their food. She was ignored by everyone but Mr. McIntyre, who occasionally glanced her way to make sure she was okay. That she was, busy cleaning her plate.

Seven people sat at the table – Madame La Framboise, the host; First Lieutenant Spencer, commander of Fort Mackinac; Mr. Niall McIntyre, the Irish fisherman who rented a room in the house; Mr. Brendan Sterling the stablemaster; Mother; Amelia; and Gichi. Mother and Amelia had served the food and then sat down to join in at Madame's invitation. Usually when there were outside guests, they served and ate in the kitchen with Gichi. But Madame always invited them to sit with her when there were no guests. The commander had been a last-minute addition; everyone else lived there and felt comfortable with informality.

Gichi helped take empty plates into the kitchen when everyone was done, and she helped serve the rice pudding. Her mouth watered at the mere sight of the delicacy. She was the first to finish hers.

The commander didn't linger after dessert, pushing his chair back and standing to politely excuse himself. "I hate to stay away from the fort for too long, especially on a blustery night like this. The deeper the snow becomes, the more difficult it is to walk up that bluff." His bushy eyebrows shot up at the mention of trekking up the bluff's long, upward path in this weather. "Therefore, I take my leave. Madame and ladies," he added, bowing in the direction of the women, "thank you for the excellent meal. Gichi ..." once again he turned his attention to her and she snapped to attention "... and gentlemen, it's been a pleasure. Sir," he addressed Mr. McIntyre, "everyone at the fort looks forward to more of your whitefish and trout, as soon as this beastly weather allows."

Madame walked him to the front hall where his winter-wear hung on a hall tree. Those left at the table sat still until they heard the front door close behind him.

"Ladies, lass, gentleman, may I please excuse meself as well? I'm going out this evening and I need to go try to look presentable." Mr. McIntyre jested, Gichi figured, because he always looked presentable as far as she was concerned.

Gichi caught her mother and Amelia exchanging a glance as if they didn't want him to go out. Why? she wondered. He usually went to the shore where men made large fires in the evening and drank whiskey while they merrily told tales that got taller as the evening went on. Sometimes, though, she knew he did something else. She'd heard Mother and Amelia talk about it.

"Certainly, Niall," Mother finally said. "We'll take it out of your hide tomorrow for not helping clean up," she teased, lightening the mood.

He got up, playfully pinched Gichi's cheek, and left the dining room, his boots clopping on the stairs out in the hall as he went up to his rented room.

"Gichi, mon bébé, let's wash the dishes and get you to bed," Mother said.

Later, alone on her cot in their small bedroom, she remembered today was the solstice d'hiver, the winter solstice. The shortest day of the year. Tomorrow would be the beginning of a new season and soon it would be a new year, one that might bring a new school to the island. She would refuse to go, of course. School meant sitting in a room all day instead of being outdoors, listening to the teacher talk and writing things down on paper. Nothing could possibly be more boring.

4

LAKE HURON, JUNE 21, 2022

"I'm so glad you're here with me. This is exciting, and we all know I've needed some excitement in my tragically boring life." Wanda dragged out those last three words for comical effect, even though they were true.

Wanda and her friends sat on the top deck of the ferry taking them to Mackinac Island. It wasn't crowded, so they had a row to themselves with an empty seat in-between each of them, their arms thrown up along the backs of the extra seats and their legs languidly stretched out in front of them. Their faces shielded with sunhats and sunglasses, their rolled-up short sleeves let their arms soak up the warmth of the sun, which peeked in and out from behind weightless white clouds that moseyed lazily across the vivid blue sky.

"This *is* exciting," Gale agreed. "It couldn't be a more ideal day."

Dawn closed her eyes and let her head lob back, exposing her neck to the sky in a display of trust. "Smell that fresh lake water. I never knew it smelled so good. I don't ever want to go back. Can I live on this boat?"

"Sure," Wanda asserted. "But I'm pretty certain the captain will put you to work."

Dawn chortled. "Yeah. Probably. Guess I'd better wait until we get there to see if I can hide away on the island where no one can find me."

"What about your husband and child?" Gale asked. "Remember them?"

"Oh, yeah. I forgot. I love them and need to go back to them – eventually."

The ferry hit the wake from another boat and sprinkled them with lake water.

"That feels good!" Wanda rubbed the droplets up and down her arms.

Gale stood, cast her hat aside, and walked to the rail. More spray, heavier this time, showered her upper body. She threw her head back and laughed like a little kid.

Wanda and Dawn joined her, and the three friends frolicked like girls in the breeze and spray and sunlight for the fifteen minutes it took to arrive on Mackinac Island. They disembarked with their hair disheveled, their clothes damp and in disarray, and their spirits lifted.

In the flurry of passengers gathering around the large luggage racks that were hauled off the boat, Wanda turned around and bumped smack dab into the swarthy chest of a man.

"Oh! Oh. I'm so sorry," she apologized.

"No, it was me. I was looking the other way. My luggage ..."

They'd stepped back from one another, and Wanda's breath caught in her throat as she lost the ability to speak. She looked into dazzling denim blue eyes. A sudden blush rose from somewhere around her heart and flared upward to color her cheeks give-away pink. It also traveled south to stir her longing. That hadn't happened since ... well, it had been so long she didn't remember when.

He'd spontaneously reached out to wrap a hand around her arm, seeing she'd been knocked off balance. He let go. She felt abandoned.

He let loose with a dazzling smile. About her age, he had what romance novels called a "chiseled" face and it looked like a "chiseled" body under jeans and a polo shirt. A touch of silver fringed his neatly cut hair at the temples. He carried a backpack and a pack that looked like it would hold a professional camera.

Before either of them got in another word, a blustery man in a suit intervened. "Mr. McIntyre! So glad you made it." The man stuck out his hand to shake and led Mr. McIntyre away. But her dream man turned around and graced her with one more smile before being shuffled into an elegant, red, Grand Hotel carriage.

Mesmerized by the exchange, Wanda gazed at the retreating carriage until reality smacked her back to the situation at hand.

"Bay View Inn!" a dockporter shouted, shattering her spell as he sought out the visitors whose luggage he'd be transporting on his bike.

Another dockporter hollered, "Island House!"

Dawn stepped up next to Wanda. Distracted by her phone, she hadn't noticed the man. "Those aren't where we're staying," she said as she punched at her phone. "The one I found online while we were in the car had been booked up, but they'd just had a three-room cancellation. Everything else on the island is booked but it seems like this was meant to be. Let me see ..." she scrolled "... it's...."

"Harbor View Inn!"

"That's us!" Dawn raised her hand like a school-kid and trotted over to the man. "Hi Sean," she greeted the dockporter, reading off his name badge. "We heard how y'all have to carry everything on your bike because there aren't any cars, so we left most of our stuff behind. We only brought a few things."

A gaggle of people grabbed their bags off the large carts. There were day-trippers, long-termers, couples, families, and a number of dogs. Dog-lovers Wanda, Gale, and Dawn momentarily became distracted by a husky, a golden retriever, and a mutt. After the overload of cuteness, they turned their attention back to finding their luggage.

Each of the three women had one small roller bag and one smaller accessory bag, six pieces in all. They pointed them out to Sean and he gathered the bags together to load onto his bicycle.

"Wait, that's too much," Wanda realized. "You can't carry all that on a bike. We can roll our bigger bags to the inn. It isn't far, is it?" She hadn't been to the island in years and didn't remember the locations of the many inns.

Sean was a burly kid, college age, with whirly hair and a cock-eyed grin. "No problem, ladies. I've got this."

They watched in awe as Sean piled their bigger bags onto the front of his bicycle and the smaller ones on the back, balancing them perfectly and securing them with bungie cords. "This way." He rolled his top-heavy bike out of the dockside loading area and onto the street. The women followed. He hopped on his bike and pointed. "Go past the fort; it's the two-story white house on the left, with the two-story porch. Saint Anne's Church is on the other side. You can't miss it. Your bags will be waiting in your rooms." He put his foot on the petal, poised to go.

"Wait! Here." It was Gale who realized they might not see him back at the inn. She pulled a five-dollar bill out of her purse and handed it to him.

"Oh, my, yes." Dawn followed suit.

Wanda felt like an idiot for not thinking of it. "Thank you so much." She handed over a bill.

Sean stuffed the cash into his shirt pocket, let loose with that adorable grin, and rode on down the street, expertly dodging bicycles commandeered by inexperienced visitors with the power to mangle his balancing act and horse-drawn carriages with the power to obliterate him.

"This place is amazing!" Gale marveled as a carriage sauntered by. "Those horses are magnificent."

"Look there!" Dawn pointed.

A horse-drawn cart loaded with Amazon Prime packages pulled over and parked. The driver hopped down to make deliveries.

"Well, I'll be. I've never seen the likes of that," Dawn said. "No blue Prime van with a swoop on the side." She swiped the logo in the air.

They ambled on down the sidewalk, peeking in the windows of shops, pubs, and restaurants and relishing the ambiance of being in a small, Victorian-era town with no motorized vehicles.

"It's like going back over a hundred years." Wanda took in a deep breath of what felt like renewed life. "That's what I always loved about it here when I was a kid."

"Wanda, I saw you talking to a really hot guy on the dock," Gale said, abruptly changing the subject. "Who was he?"

"I don't know."

"What? Dang. I missed it," Dawn groused. "What do you mean, you 'don't know'? Who was he?"

"I don't know. The man who met him called him 'Mr. McIntyre'."

"Well, that Mr. McIntyre is gorgeous," Gale said, making it three syllables for emphasis – gor-ge-ous.

"You two have been reading too many romance novels," Wanda claimed. She didn't mention that she'd already figured he'd make a good cover for a romance novel. A sexy, swoony, midlife love story.

"Oh, honey, there's no such thing as 'too many romance novels.' Now, I want to hear more about this man." Dawn wouldn't relent.

"I don't know any more. I only glanced at him for a second."

"With a guy like that, a second is all you need," Gale tittered.

"Did you notice his shoes?" Dawn wanted to know.

"For heaven's sake, no. Why would I look at his shoes? Of course, you would notice that."

"I always notice shoes. Y'all can tell a lot about a man by his shoes."

"And by the size of his feet." Gale snickered.

Dawn nudged Gale. "Ha. Good one, another good reason to pay attention to shoes. I wish you'd noticed. I need to know before I know if you should talk to him again."

Wanda looked down at her sneakers. "Well, he undoubtedly outclasses me."

"No, he doesn't," Gale insisted.

Uncomfortable with the direction this conversation had taken, Wanda pointed and said, "There's the fort I told you about." The fort had come into view, regally sitting atop a bluff, its iconic white walkway a long diagonal wall up to the white-walled fortress. "And this is the park underneath it with the statue of Jacques Marquette.

He's the French missionary who's credited with being one of the first to explore this region in the 1600s. He was on a mission to bring religion to the natives."

"Didn't they already have religion?" Gale queried. "Their own?"

"Yeah, good point. Oh my! Look at the lilac bushes!" Their attention riveted to the lush bushes in the park and lining the street on both sides of this more residential part of town. "They're in full bloom. And look over here," she said, gesturing across the street from the park. "That's the marina that makes me drool over all those yachts. We'll look at that after we get settled."

"I want to tour the fort," Gale said.

"I want a yacht," Dawn said.

"And I want to find Gichi and her mystery friend," Wanda said. "But first, let's go smell the lilacs." She jaunted across the lawn of the park to a lilac bush in full bloom and stuck her nose into a blossom, savoring the aroma.

Gale and Dawn followed suit.

"That smell!" Gale said after inhaling deeply. "Holy moly, that's wonderful!"

Dawn did her own inhaling. "It makes me feel like I'm floatin', it's so beautiful. This light purple color is so pretty."

Pleased that her friends were falling in love with the island, which she already loved so dearly, Wanda wandered over to another nearby lilac bush, this one a purplish-red magenta. She buried her nose in a sweet blossom and felt heady as a result. She backed up a few steps and did it again with another bloom.

After a healthy hit of beauty and aroma, they continued on down the sidewalk toward their inn.

Dawn, as it turned out, wasn't about to let go of their earlier conversation. "Listen, Wanda. You're single. You could at least strike up a conversation to find out if a man is available."

"What? Are you out of your mind? What was I supposed to say? 'Excuse me, I know we've only met for three seconds, but are you married'?"

"Sure, why not?"

"Yes," Gale insisted. "It's time, Wanda. You can't hide from life forever. I know you want to find those dead people. But it's time to pay attention to the living, too. Come on, where's that Towanda we've teased you about so often?"

Fried Green Tomatoes was a favorite movie of this trio of best friends. Towanda was the character Idgie's alter-ego, the name she used when feeling empowered.

"I don't feel like Towanda right now. Not yet. It isn't time."

"Not time?" Gale rolled her eyes so dramatically her whole head rolled with them. "Why not?"

"Because, well, you know, ah, I don't know."

"That's right. You don't know. But we do."

"Yes, ma'am," Dawn added. "Stick with us. We'll fix you right up."

"Oh, lordy, I'm in so much trouble."

"Yup. Good trouble." Gale laughed.

With that they made their way to the Harbor View Inn and checked into their rooms, which were side-by-side-by-side. Their luggage was indeed waiting for them in their rooms like trusty Sean said they would be.

Immediately feeling at home in her lovely blue-and-white room and glad for the escape, Wanda plopped down spread eagle on the bed and let out a long exhale of pent-up air.

5

MACKINAC ISLAND, DECEMBER 21, 1822

Gichi held her breath as she slipped off her cot that was in the small room she shared with her mother and Amelia, next to the kitchen at the back of the house. She'd tried to sleep, truly she had, but the low voices in the kitchen woke her up. Instead of only her mother and Amelia talking like usual, a man had joined them. That man being Mr. McIntyre, Gichi couldn't resist eavesdropping.

She tiptoed to the door, opened it a crack, and peeked out. There he was sitting at the table with the women, his back to her. Tall with broad shoulders, even from behind he presented an imposing figure on the small kitchen chair, like an eagle perched on a fencepost. Gichi could tell he'd combed his dark, unruly hair. Dressed differently than most days, tonight he wore his Sunday go-to-church clothes – pressed pants, a striped shirt, and a vest – which could only mean one thing. He was going to see Miss Rebecca Wright.

His big outstretched hand covered a small red box that sat on the table.

"So you see, me loves, I need help tying a pretty bow with this ribbon." He pulled a red ribbon out of the breast pocket of his vest.

"Madame said I could use this. These fisherman's hands of mine are too clumsy for such fine work. I want this to be a very special Christmas gift. I'm giving it to Miss Wright tonight, along with my proposal of marriage."

Gichi gasped and watched Mother and Amelia inhale quick breaths. They struggled not to offend their friend. Her mother recovered first.

"Oh, Niall, dear, don't you think it's a bit soon to propose marriage?" Mother patted his hand as if to try to prod it off the box. Mother's English was slightly stilted with Odawa and French influence, but she'd grown up with English, too, so knew lots of good words. Gichi strove to be like that someday with lots of good words, even if she had to silently keep them in her head. "Perhaps you could take some time to think about it," Mother suggested to Mr. McIntyre. "You have plenty of time."

"Yes, that's a good idea." Amelia rushed to add. "It'll be months before spring when the ice breaks and Miss Wright will be able to leave the island. She isn't going anywhere soon."

"No, ladies." He spoke with undeniable conviction. "Thank you for your sage advice, but I've made up my mind. I love Miss Wright. I believe she loves me, too. I want to ask for her hand in marriage."

"But Niall, you've only been in this country for six months." Mother's voice became strained with pleading. "And you're still young. There needn't be any rush."

"Truer words were never spoken," Amelia chorused. "How old are you, Niall?"

"Almost twenty. Plenty old to be getting married." He'd balked, and then calmed down.

"I know what you're doing. You're trying to protect me like a mother because you're my friends and me own ma is so far away. I thank you for your concern. But I don't need protecting. I'm a grown man and know what I'm doing."

Mother and Amelia had both leaned forward in earnestness. Now they gave up and slouched back into their chairs.

"Well, then, you may as well show us what you've got there," Mother said.

"I couldn't afford a gold engagement ring with a gemstone," he explained, "but I bought this from Mr. Schmidt. He used to be a jeweler back in Germany."

He opened the small box and the women stared in what could be mistaken for astonishment, but Gichi knew horror when she saw it. As hard as she tried, she couldn't see what was in the box. Not a ring, obviously, but what? She might burst with curiosity.

"What did Madame say about this?" Mother turned the conversation back to Madame La Framboise, her employer and his landlord, known as the First Lady of Mackinac Island. Her success in the fur trade made her well respected and seldom challenged.

Mr. McIntyre hesitated but garnered resolve. "She had some misgivings, but I assured her I feel secure in my decision."

"And?" Mother wouldn't relent. Gichi knew that all too well.

"And she told me she feared I would be disappointed. I look forward to proving her wrong, as much as I respect her opinion. But in matters of the heart, I believe she is mistaken. At least this one time."

The silence that followed pressed down so heavily Gichi could feel it on her skin.

Her mother sighed and took the ribbon in hand, and Amelia slid the box across the table to her. She handily tied the ribbon around the box, fashioned a bow, and fluffed it up prettily.

"It's perfect. Thank you, me loves." Mr. McIntyre popped out of his chair and pulled on his heavy wool coat that hung on a peg by the fireplace. He grabbed the wool scarf his mother back home in Eire had knitted for him and wrapped it snugly around his neck.

He had told Gichi the story about how each fisherman clan in Eire had its own cable pattern that the women knitted into family members' scarves and sweaters. Gichi thought that a wonderful tradition. A person could tell what family someone was from by looking at the design on their clothes.

When he turned back to pick up the box, he faced in Gichi's direction, his smile so radiant she could suddenly understand why women called him handsome. He took the box and disappeared out the back door.

Mother and Amelia frowned in unison.

"We'd better be ready to take care of a drunkard when he comes home," her mother said.

"No doubt," Amelia agreed.

"I'll get a bucket and put it at his bedside."

"Good idea."

As they blew out the candles, Mother's head unexpectedly jerked around to look straight at Gichi staring through the crack in the door.

"Mademoiselle Gichigama Geneviève St. Croix! What are you doing listening in at that door?" Gichi knew that stern voice. That and the use of her full name – the formal French title, her given Odawa name, her father's mother's name, and her father's French-Canadian last name – meant she was in big trouble. Experience told her big trouble was not good.

Bravely, she pushed the door open all the way, straightened her backbone, and lifted her chin in defiance. She pointed at herself.

"You," her mother said, practiced at reading her daughter's gestures.

Gichi nodded. She jabbed a finger at the ceiling.

"You have something to say about Mr. McIntyre's room."

Gichi shook her head and made a chopping motion.

"Chop it off. Oh, not room. Mr. McIntyre himself."

Gichi nodded vigorously, then shook her head while cutting her flattened hands through the air.

"He should not do something."

The girl nodded again, put her hands up with floppy wrists, strutted on tiptoe, and cocked her head from side to side as she tottered around the room.

"Oh! He shouldn't go to see Miss Wright."

Now Gichi made the motions of opening the jewelry box. She shook her head.

"He shouldn't propose to Miss Wright."

Gichi nodded with wild abandon.

Taken aback, the women glared at her.

"Gichi," Amelia cackled, "that was a perfect impression of her."

Then both women fell into a fit of laughter.

Gichi sighed with relief as "big trouble" was forgotten.

6

MACKINAC ISLAND, JUNE 21, 2022

W anda slid out of bed, went to the window, and opened
the blinds. From her second-story room, she could see
a lighthouse blinking on a tiny rock island not far away
in Lake Huron. The winking glow soothed her troubled nerves.

Even though it was midnight, a horse-drawn carriage noncha-
lantly rode by on the street out front. She'd opened the window
earlier to catch the balmy breeze off the lake, and the cadenced clip-
clop of the horse's hooves further calmed her down.

She'd been restless, unable to sleep. Her life as she'd known it for
twenty-five years was all out of sorts. No, she realized, dissolved.
Gone.

She needed a new life.

Her mind refused to rest until she figured out what that new life
might be. Back home in Georgia she'd been busy readying their
house for sale, packing, cleaning, repairing, and doing yard work.
She'd kept herself busy, busy, busy. But here she was in one of her
favorite places, Mackinac Island, with no mundane distractions. The
fresh water of the Great Lakes, verdant thick woods, vibrant lush
gardens, and a Victorian-era town surrounded her. She needed to
allow it to bring her peace of mind.

But as her mind moved past distractions and came home to itself, what it found there disturbed her. She didn't know where she belonged anymore.

Her husband Ralph – ex-husband she reminded herself – had insisted she start a business as a housecleaner because she'd always taken such good care of their house. What he didn't say was he hoped she'd make enough money to relieve him of paying alimony, because he had a lot of expenses coming up with his new, younger wife, being pregnant with twins. He'd always made good money as an airline executive but had somehow managed to squander it. Wanda's lawyer had squeezed out a pittance in alimony.

Wanda's job as Ralph's unofficial assistant was caput and she was getting next to nothing for it. For years she'd done most of his voluminous paperwork and created all his training programs, which he always brought home to her because he didn't want anyone at work to know he didn't know how or didn't want to do them. She'd edited and rewritten every proposal he'd ever turned in. She'd hosted countless dinners for his supervisors and their spouses to give him an edge.

It chapped her ass that after twenty-five years of doing a big chunk of his vice-head-honcho work for him, he pushed her to clean houses.

Wanda didn't want to clean other people's houses.

Her mother wanted her to go into real estate sales.

She didn't want to be a realtor.

Her daughter suggested wedding planning.

Really? All those bridezillas? No.

Gale and Dawn never pressed her, which she adored about them. They simply stood by while she bounced around, at midlife no less, trying to figure out this life thing. No matter where she landed, she knew they'd be there to catch her if she stumbled into the abyss.

She went over to the ancient family Bible she'd placed on a side table and opened it again. She'd studied the unfamiliar names for an hour before going to bed. The handwriting alone intrigued her. Knowing that her own ancestors' hands had touched those crinkled pages seemed extraordinary, forming a bond to kin she would never know. A search on ancestry.com helped her to find a few of them, but most were still an enigma. She considered firing up her laptop and going at it again.

But an owl hooted outside, entreating her to forget the past for now and pay attention to this very moment. A magical, mysterious night awaited her outdoors.

She shucked her nightie, threw on shorts and a tank top, and shoved her feet into flip-flops. The urge to get outside to be in the middle of such a majestic black night had become overwhelming. Once she reached the out-of-doors, the crisp night air revived her. She felt alive, even hopeful for no reason she could discern. She turned right on Main Street and marveled at the magnificent Victorian-era cottages along the way.

She felt as if the island belonged to her and her alone. Well, for a while, anyway.

When she reached Marquette Park below Fort Mackinac on its bluff, a gaggle of ebullient young adults passed by on the other side of the street in front of the marina. She assumed they were island workers, perhaps college kids here for the summer. They attempted to be quiet, as open windows at cottages and inns were common in the nighttime because air conditioning wasn't often needed this far north, but their happiness slipped out a bit noisily a couple of times. One would laugh boisterously, and another would shush them so loudly it became comical.

A pang of jealousy struck over their youth and liveliness and hopeful futures. If she could figure out her future, she'd be all set.

She got to the main section of town, where shop abounded, before she saw anyone else. Two men and two women rode by on their bikes, waving hello as they headed west on the continuation of Main Street that surrounded the entire island. Wanda had read it was M-185, the only state road in the country that didn't allow motor vehicles. At 8.2 miles long on the flat shore, it was an easy ride. She remembered riding it with her parents when she was a kid and decided that she and the girls must do it, too.

Walking along without running into anyone else, she entered a secluded world of enchanting solitude. Past the shops were more Victorian-era cottages, private homes and inns, magical fairytale manors looming in the dark of night. A dim light shone in a window here and there. A porch light occasionally cropped up. But mostly the domiciles slumbered, their decades of dreams and stories pressing at the walls in a desperate need to be told.

She strode to the middle of the street and looked around, an epiphany having struck. She wanted to discover and tell those stories. Who had built these homes? What had their hopes and dreams been? Were they happy? Heartbroken? Who had lived on the island before these places existed? Did the island bring them comfort? What was her own connection to this enigmatic place, her link to a woman named Gichi and an unnamed friend, who apparently had lived here?

"Pfft," she whispered, shaking her head to dismiss the crazy idea. "Like I could ever do all that. But at least maybe I can find Gichi and her secret admirer."

Stepping across the street to a public lawn that met the shore, she wandered down to the water and watched as gentle waves lapped at the pebbled beach. She could feel her heart attune itself to the rhythm of the waves. It soothed her even more, guiding her into an almost meditative state. The starry sky with its slit of a crescent moon completed the peacefulness that infused her body. Indeed, her very soul.

That was when she saw him again, the man from the dock. Mr. McIntyre. He didn't see her. He stood on the shore about thirty yards ahead of her, his camera on a tripod and pointed at the Mackinac Bridge that stood off in the distance. The bridge that connected the upper and lower peninsulas of Michigan shone brightly in the night, its graceful form adorned with decorative lights. He leaned forward with his eye at the viewfinder.

But then, as if sensing her presence, he backed away from his camera and turned to look right at her. Neither of them moved, frozen in place.

Suddenly self-conscious and feeling as if she'd disturbed his solitude, she threw him a little wave and turned to go.

"Wait," he called as he took a few steps toward her.

"Oh, I'm sorry. I didn't mean to intrude."

"You're not. Really. It's okay."

"No, I need to go. Sorry. 'Bye."

She scurried away before he could object again. And before Gale's and Dawn's admonitions could get to her.

By the time she reached the main part of town again, she derided herself for acting so foolishly. "You promised yourself you'd stop apologizing all the time, you dimwit," she muttered to herself. Then she derided herself for deriding herself. "And you promised yourself you'd stop telling yourself you'd done something wrong. That's the ghost of Ralph-of-Christmas-and-every-other-day-of-my-life past haunting you. Remember?" She muttered some more until reaching the Harbor View Inn, where she sat on the front steps for a while to take in the starry sky and to force herself to stop muttering to herself.

Eventually, her eyelids became heavy and her body begged for repose. She ambled back to her room and finally fell fast asleep.

7

DECEMBER 21, 1822

Sleep proved impossible. Gichi's eyes refused to close. Mr. McIntyre was out there getting his heart broken into pieces. She needed to be there to help her friend. She had no idea how to help a grownup with a shattered heart, but there must be something she could do.

Her mother's deep breathing and Amelia's soft snore told her it was safe to get up. As quietly as a mouse, she left their room and went into the kitchen. Listening carefully, she didn't hear a peep. She sat down in the rocking chair by the fire, which had burned down to embers, to put on her moccasins. Everyone left their moccasins and boots under the pegs where they hung their wraps and coats. Next she donned her cap, fur wrap, and mittens. Tiptoeing to the back door, her hand made it all the way to the knob when ...

"Gichi," a raspy voice whispered, causing the girl to jump with fright. "Where do you think you are going?"

She turned around to come face to face with none other than Madame La Framboise herself. Gichi's whole head trembled, as if she had no control of her skull, as she attempted to shake it to say she didn't know.

"You're going out to look for Mr. McIntyre, aren't you?" The tall, stately woman had bent down to get face to face with the girl. She too was bundled up for the out-of-doors.

There was no use lying to Madame. She was so smart she could probably read minds like a medicine woman. Gichi nodded yes.

"Well ..." Madame looked around to make sure no one else was listening "... so am I. You need to go back to bed. There's no need for both of us to go out in this storm. Besides, this is no night for a girl to be out there. I'll see to it he comes home. Now scoot. Go to bed." She shooed at Gichi with her hands.

Gichi stared up at the beautiful Odawa woman – her godmother, her mother's employer and friend, their benefactor – and knew she should obey. For a moment she thought she might. Madame watched as she went to the bedroom door and obediently put her hand on the knob as if to enter. Madame nodded approval. Gichi nodded in return.

Madame left the house and quietly closed the door behind her. Gichi waited for as long as she could stand it. She strode across the room, opened the door, and poked her head outside. A blast of frigid air struck her face. She swiped at the resulting tears in her eyes. Madame's frame was already lost in the thick wall of snow that fell from the sky. Gichi imitated Madame's quiet exit and turned right to head for town, following the woman's ghostly figure ahead of her. She didn't know where they were going, but Madame's confident stride said she knew. Gichi trotted along behind, her curiosity swelling with each step.

Dome-shaped bark-wood huts, each with a hole in the top for smoke from the indoor fire to escape, where the Indians lived, and white people's wood-slat shanties, with crude stone chimneys, stood like ghosts in the dark of night. People went to bed early during these short days of winter.

From behind Gichi could see that Madame scanned the streets and the shore, her head turning from side to side, but she didn't see what she sought. She walked inland a block and went to the American Fur Trading Company building. Candlelight shone in one of the windows. Gichi had walked by the long, imposing place many times but had never been inside. Madame did not hesitate to open a side door and slip inside. Driven by snow and wind, Gichi followed right behind.

Madame had made it half-way across the pitch-black room when she turned upon hearing the door open and close. "Gichi!" she whispered, shaking her head. She put out a hand. Gichi took it and her godmother protectively drew Gichi into the fold of her cape. Together they stood stone still listening to voices in the next room.

Madame put a finger to her lips to indicate "quiet," then realized the senselessness of the act. Tenderly, she placed that finger on Gichi's lips, as if blessing them, then turned her attention to the quarrel in the next room. The door between the two rooms was closed, so Madame led Gichi to it and they pressed their ears to the wood.

"Me love, is it that I have no money? I've told you I intend to make my fortune here in America." Gichi had never heard Mr. McIntyre use such a pathetically pleading tone.

"Oh, really? How? You have no education, no status, no connections. I can't believe you thought I would ever consider marrying someone like you. You're a fisherman, for God's sake. And Irish to boot." Miss Wright's voice was that of a heathen.

"But, Rebecca, you said you loved me."

His voice had become so soft the eavesdroppers pressed their ears more tightly to the door.

"Of course I did. That's what one says when in the throes of love-making. You're an incredibly handsome man, Niall, although quite unrefined. Surely you know you are sexually appealing. No doubt other woman have wanted to bed you."

"Perhaps, but I would never do such a thing without intending marriage. I believe lovemaking cleaves us together in the eyes of God. It was a symbol of our love for one another. A promise to marry."

Silence hung in the air until Miss Wright growled, "Oh my God. You really believe that? You're more naïve than I could have imagined. We had a tryst, Niall. That's all. It's over."

"But how can I live with the fact that I've ruined you for another? Who will want to marry you now that you have been with a man?"

"Oh, don't worry about that. I've plenty of suitors. And if it makes you feel better, you weren't the first. Or second or third, to be honest. There's no need for guilt."

"Rebecca! Surely that is not true."

"Surely it is. Well, I need to get back upstairs to our quarters, and you need to go." She abruptly changed the subject, coldly dismissing him. "My father said I could talk to you for fifteen minutes but that's all. Here. Take your little gift. I don't want it. It wouldn't be very nice of me to keep it now, would it? You can give it to your little wife some-day. I'm sure you'll be married with a passel of children running around, living your fisherman's life. I can't even imagine such a thing."

They heard fleeting footsteps on stairs as Miss Wright turned her back on her lover and escaped, leaving Niall McIntyre with a shat-tered heart. All was quiet for a few excruciatingly long minutes. Gichi held her breath. What was he going to do? Suddenly, quick, heavy footfall headed for their door.

Madame grabbed Gichi's arm and yanked her aside in time to save them from being pummeled by the door as it burst open. Mr. McIntyre stormed through the room, thrust open the outside door like a bear attacking a hunter, and disappeared into the night. The gale outside sent snow whirling into the room behind him, as if the gods of winter approved of the man's wrath.

In his fury, Mr. McIntyre hadn't noticed them cowering behind the door. They scurried out to follow, losing him at times in the blinding blizzard, but eventually spying him on the shore. Lake Huron was sporadically frozen, its massive burgeoning icefield buried in a foot of snow. They stood behind a tree, hardly hiding anymore, and watched their friend from behind.

Facing the lake, he howled like a dying beast. His tortured call mingled with the bluster of the storm, rising to dissolve into the winter sky. He took the little red box out of his pocket and pitched it out onto the lake as far as the wind would allow. It looked like a blood stain in the snow until disappearing as falling snow buried it.

His shoulders shook; he burrowed his fists into his eyes; his sobs could be imagined if not heard. Gichi had never seen a man cry. She didn't know what to do. Should they go try to comfort him? She looked up at Madame for guidance.

Madame shook her head. "No, sweet girl. This he must handle on his own. He must face his sorrow. Only then will he ever know joy again. But here's what I will do: I'll get Bernard to check on him from afar, to make sure he doesn't get frozen stiff in the snow. How's that?"

Bernard, Mr. Sterling the stablemaster to Gichi, slept in the loft of Madame's carriage house behind her house. He and Mr. McIntyre had become friends. Gichi nodded. That was a good plan.

She took Madame's hand as they trudged home through snow-drifts. Turning her head as far as possible to look back, Mr. McIntyre soon disappeared into a cloud of white, fading away like a fragile angel.

Madame must have had a similar thought because instead of going straight home, they went to Ste. Anne's Church next door. There Madame bowed and made the sign of the cross over her chest. Gichi did the same. Then Madame lit an altar candle and they pulled down the kneel pads to pray. Gichi closed her eyes then opened one to venture a glimpse at Madame. The woman's eyes were closed while her lips moved in silent prayer.

"Gichi, close your eyes and pray," she said without opening her eyes.

Gichi squeezed her eyes shut. Amongst all else, Madame could see with her eyes closed!

The girl didn't know what to ask of God. She had no experience with broken hearts, so asked that Mr. McIntyre feel better in the morning. Surely, a good night's sleep would make it all better. That's what Mother always told her when she was feeling sad, and it always worked.

8

JUNE 22, 2022

Coffee.

If Wanda didn't get some soon, she might die. She rolled out of bed, threw on some clothes, splashed water on her face, and gave her mouth a quick once-over with her toothbrush. She ventured halfway down the stairs when the savory smell of the elixir of life hit her. She would live, after all.

Gale and Dawn already sat in the breakfast room enjoying coffee and croissants at a small, round table where an empty chair awaited Wanda. Being the end of the breakfast hour, everyone else had come and gone, so the room was all theirs.

"There she is, our sweet sleepyhead," Dawn announced.

"Mornin' girls." Wanda struggled to force her tongue to work while she fixed herself a generous cup of coffee from the side table stocked with breakfast goodies.

"You okay?" Gale asked. "You slept late for you. You're usually the first one up."

"Yeah, I'm fine." She gulped from her mug and joined them. "I was up in the night. It was so beautiful out I took a walk." She slugged down more coffee.

"Oh, wow, wasn't that kinda spooky?" Dawn asked.

"No, not at all. It was peaceful." Wanda took a moment to clear the remains of muddled sleep from her brain to find the right words. "Inspirational. Freeing. It was like my mind opened up." She emptied her cup and got up for a refill.

"Oh dear, that sounds serious. I'm glad I was asleep," Gale jibed good-naturedly. "What did your mind find when it opened all the way up like that?" she added, turning more serious.

"I'm not sure yet. It's not like I came up with any answers, I just stopped torturing myself with the same questions over and over. Like why did my husband have an affair and leave me to marry a ditzy, young, flight attendant."

"Because he's a flamin' asshole," Dawn stated flatly.

"You were a flight attendant once, remember?" Gale said. "You weren't a ditz, though. And you gave it up because he wanted you to. He wanted a wife at home to cater to his every need."

Dawn muttered, "Dumb-butt wanted a mommy."

"I know, I know," Wanda moaned. "We've figured all that out. But last night it was if that question became irrelevant. The question is: why did I let someone – anyone, husband or otherwise – talk me into giving up a career I loved? Why did I devote my entire life to my kids and husband, all of whom are now gone with the wind, instead of giving myself some space, too? I mean, you know I love my kids and new grandchild more than life itself. But I let their lives eat mine up. That's on me, not them."

Her friends didn't so much as blink. Neither spoke. Their agreement filled the silence.

"Last night while I was looking out at the lake in the darkness, I felt such a connection to the past, whatever that might be. I felt a 'calling' – I guess that's what people call it – to find out more, not only about my family's history and this person named Gichi. I want to do something with history but have no idea what."

Purposely, she deigned to tell them about running into the "hot" man again and her namsy-pansy chicken-shit flight away from him. She didn't need any more love lessons so early in the morning.

"Well," Dawn said, "you certainly have a lot of options if you want to work with 'history'. I mean, there are millions of years to cover. There must be something in there you can do."

Gale swiped her phone, leaned in conspiratorially, and read off her screen. "How about starting here? I've found a genealogist right here on the island. She specializes in island family searches but does online searches all over the world, too. It says she knows local archives – county, town, church, state park, military, private. Sounds like she can find anything as long as it exists. Her name is Alexandra Ames." She held up her phone. "Shall we call her right now?"

"Sure." Wanda felt totally awake now, excited at this possibility.

Gale punched the number and handed the phone to Wanda.

Alexandra Ames answered immediately. Wanda told her who she sought, and after a lengthy conversation she hung up.

"She's amazing. She's usually booked up in advance but has a last-minute cancellation, so we can meet with her for a little while this afternoon. Assuming you want to come."

"You can bet money on that," Gale slapped the table, as if anteing her cash.

"Of course we're goin', darlin'," Dawn chirped.

"Good. We already know from that DNA test I took that I'm mostly Scottish and Irish, with some Norwegian thrown in, but it's the slice of Native American they found that throws me. Maybe I'll find out about that this afternoon. That Gichi has to be connected somehow."

They'd finished their croissants and coffees and stood to clean up their trash.

"I know what we can do in the meantime," Wanda informed her friends. "There were people riding bikes around the island in the middle of the night. We must do it right now. It's an island tradition."

Gale's eyes widened. "Ah, Wanda, I haven't ridden a bike in a hundred and fifty years."

"Me, either," Dawn said, "but only about a hundred and forty years, cuz I'm younger than y'all."

"Yeah, yeah, we know," Wanda chided. "Wait till we're old and feeble and you're the only one around to take care of us. If you don't, we'll tell all your secrets."

"No you won't. Y'all won't remember them by then."

They ribbed each other and laughed as they left the inn and crossed the street to go to a bike rental place. There they got three ladies' old-timey bikes with wicker baskets and no brake handles. Wanda hopped on first, rode in a circle in front of the store, and skidded to a stop to show off her skills.

"You press back on your pedals to brake, like when we were kids."

"Oh, I can do that," Gale grinned like a kid as she tried out her bike. Wobbly at first, she straightened up and rode on down the street. Her confidence soaring, she let go of the handlebars and threw her arms up for the moment it took to holler, "Yippee-ki-ay!"

Not to be outdone, Dawn took off, crouching down and pedaling hard at first and then sticking her legs out while bellowing, "Whoo-hoo!"

Wanda took up the rear, watching her friends' childish antics and feeling as happy as Idgie in *Fried Green Tomatoes*. "Towanda!" she bellowed.

Her friends whooped assent, and they rode away with wild abandon.

9

DECEMBER 22, 1822

Gichi did her best to remain silent as she stole out of bed once again. It was early morning but still dark as midnight. She'd hardly slept. How could she when her friend was out there in the snowstorm? She hadn't heard Mr. McIntyre's heavy footsteps on the stairs going up to his room, so she fretted about his safety. Madame said she'd send Mr. Sterling to look after him, but where was he?

In the kitchen, she felt her way in the dark as if half blind with only the smoldering embers in the fireplace providing a glint of light. She finally made her way to the pegs on the wall. Swaddled in her warm gear, she slipped out of the house to be greeted by a blue-black morning with pristine snow covering the entire world.

Pausing briefly to take in the measure of the snow, "goon" Mother called it when she used her native Odawa language, Gichi could see that her snowshoes that hung on a nail by the door would do no good. Odawa people knew how to tell the difference amongst the many types of goon, and this was too light for snowshoes, which would merely sink into the dusty drifts. She took off without them.

Stillness surrounded her. The fierce wind of the night before had fallen into slumber. What had once been houses, huts, shanties, stores, the street, and the lake all became one giant, fluffy, undulating blanket of sleeping white powder.

It was magical!

But she couldn't tarry in her awe. She must look for her friend. She walked each street and path, difficult muddy ruts in the summertime but now evened out by ice and snow. She looked for a human form covered in white. There was none. Willowy streams of smoke filtered out of the holes and chimneys of huts, shanties, and houses, remnants of fires from the night before. None had yet been stoked into blazing new fires for the new day. The small town was still asleep.

Mr. McIntyre was nowhere to be found. At least she felt comfort in that. If he wasn't outside stuck in a snowbank, he must have taken shelter somewhere. Perhaps someone took pity on him and invited him inside. He must be safely asleep like the rest of the island.

She headed for home but paused at the shoreline where he'd thrown the little red box out onto the lake. There was no hint of the thing now, long buried in snow. But a thought wound its way into her mind. What if he'd thrown an expensive gift out there in a fit of rage and sorrow, and what if he would want it back after he calmed down? Throwing money away wasn't something most people on the island could afford to do.

No, she had to be honest with herself. That wasn't the real reason. She desperately longed to know what was in the box.

The ice on the lake wasn't totally frozen yet, but it looked like a large field of white where stretches of ice were covered in mounds of snow, with rivulets of water meandering amongst them where the ice hadn't formed yet. It made a stunningly beautiful picture.

The box hadn't been thrown very far out. The opposing wind had been too strong to allow that. Should she take a chance and pray she wouldn't fall through the spotty ice? Curiosity or caution? It was a silly question to ask herself. She already knew.

Stepping carefully, trudging through snow that reached her knees, which was like wading through deep water, she made her way to the spot on the lake where she'd seen the box land. She had a good eye. Even though the ice would naturally have shifted and the lake looked the same for miles in three directions around her, she knew precisely where the box should be. She stopped, plunged her hand into the snow, and came up with the red box.

The snow beneath her feet wavered, almost causing her to lose her balance. The ice below the snow wobbled. She knew what to do. Slowly, she got down on her belly and crawled back to shore. Anyone from these parts knew that when a person stood on lake ice that cracked or broke, they should lie flat to spread their weight out over the ice rather than stand and let a foot holding all their weight poke through. She made it to shore without incident and stood up.

Looking around to make sure no one else was around, she dusted off the snow she gathered from crawling. She'd held the little box up out of harm's way the whole while, like a sacred talisman. She wiped snow off it, too, and paused as she wondered if she should open it.

She opened it. At that moment the sun, not yet crested on the horizon, reached over the edge of the earth to cast a purple predawn glow across her world, giving her a sliver of lavender light. She gasped. What lay in the box was a beautiful brass locket. Afraid to touch it, she closed the top and slipped it into her pocket.

She dashed home, hurriedly hung up her wrap, took off her snowy moccasins, and grabbed the broom to be busy sweeping the kitchen floor, her daily morning chore, by the time anyone else got up.

"Well, my child, did you find it?"

Gichi jumped, once again, at Madame's surprise presence. Was she a shapeshifter? Everywhere at all times?

Gichi didn't move a muscle. If she shook her head, she'd be lying. If she nodded, she'd be admitting she snuck out once again after being told not to.

"What was she looking for?"

Startled again, this time by her mother who stood at their bedroom door, she could see that Mother had asked the question of Madame, not her.

"The gift that Niall threw onto the lake."

"Ah, I see. Miss Wright refused it, of course?"

"Yes. At least she afforded him the courtesy of not pilfering a hard-earned gift that meant nothing to her."

"I didn't hear Niall come in. You talked to him?"

"No, I admit I went out looking for him an hour after he left the house. I feared he'd be inebriated after her rebuke of his marriage proposal. However, he was still with her. Naturally, she'd been late, apparently, as always. She must have kept him waiting for an hour."

Mother looked from Madame to Gichi. "Ah, I see. I assume that's where you went, too, Gichi, when you left your bed. I assumed you came in here to sit by the embers of the fire, as you sometimes do when you are restless in the night." Her tone was calm, not scolding.

"It's my fault," Madame interjected. "She was out here ..." Gichi watched her godmother's finesse as she did not lie but did not tell the whole truth "... and was curious about where I was going. She came with me. That's how she knew to look for the gift he tossed onto the lake. We saw him do it. He never knew we were there."

Gichi went to her wrap where it hung on the peg and took the little box out of the pocket. Carrying it in both hands, she handed it to Madame.

"I believe we've all seen what's inside," the woman said to the girl. "You found it. Therefore, it is now yours to return to Mr. McIntyre when the time is right." She handed it back to Gichi. "Bernard followed him last night, and he's sleeping in the stables. Perhaps he needs a tray with nourishment."

Mother scurried to fix the tray while Madame helped herself to tea with cream and bread with a dollop of butter. She offered some to Gichi, but the girl was too nervous to eat. Mr. Sterling came in for his breakfast but when he saw the flurry of activity, he offered to help before eating.

Gichi liked Mr. Sterling. He was a man of few words. Although short and skinny, he was strong and had a way with the horses he so clearly loved. When the tray was ready, he carried it to the stables with Gichi at his heels. He nodded for her to open the door and when she did, he handed her the tray. He nodded again and she understood that he thought it a good idea for her to deliver it by herself. She entered and heard the door close behind her.

The sight of Mr. McIntyre startled her. Sunken into a bed of hay on the floor in the empty stall by the door, his Sunday-go-to-church clothes wrinkled and dirty, with bird's nest hair, he looked like a helpless, abandoned orphan. An empty whiskey bottle lay at his side. The smell of the alcohol mingled with hay and horses permeated the air. A horse neighed, the stable dog appeared to beg her for a pet, which she supplied, and a cat meowed from somewhere in the bales of hay.

Mr. McIntyre opened his eyes and sat up.

"Ah, it's me bonny colleen, Gichi. A sight for sore eyes. Come, come. Don't be afraid. It's me myself, not the devil himself."

She set the tray down beside him.

"Sit, me love. Let's share this feast you've brought your poor, pitiful friend."

She sat on a bale, noticing for the first time that Mother had provided two cups. He poured a cup for each of them and peeled back the napkin that covered three thick slices of buttered brown bread. A small earthenware dish of some of Mother's delicious blackberry jam and a knife for spreading were included, too.

"You may be wondering ..." he said as he handed her a slice of bread he'd slathered with butter and jam "... why you have found me in such a pathetic state. Well, last night I asked a woman to be my wife and she said no. It's as simple as that. I am a rejected man, a penniless fisherman, unfit to be a husband and father. There you have it. End of story."

Gichi could see it was not the end of the story for him. His broken heart had not healed overnight. They ate their bread and jam and drank their tea in silence.

When done, Mr. McIntyre had more to say. "Gichi, me lass, you must promise me something. Will you promise?"

She nodded. She would promise him anything.

"I've come to feel like a big brother to you," he explained. "I hope you don't mind."

She shook her head. She did not mind at all. She'd wished he could be her father, but a big brother was good, too.

"You've helped me get over my longing for me family back home in Eire. I've told you before that I'm the oldest of ten leanaí, and I miss my younger sisters and brothers so much it makes my heart weep at times. I came to America to build me fortune and send money back to them. I see now that was a foolish dream, at least thinking it would happen quickly. But lass, here is what I would tell them, and because you are like a deirfiúr, a sister, to me, I will tell you. You must never, never, never let someone break your heart. Find a man who will love you truly and never do that to you. Be smarter than your old friend here. Choose your mate wisely. Will you promise me that?"

She nodded again, although not sure how to do such a thing.

He explained. "Make certain he always acknowledges you when you walk into a room or pass on the street. Make certain his tone of voice is one of kindness when he speaks to you. Make certain he is a good man who loves you and you alone. And Gichi, make sure you do the same for him."

He sighed, his gaze drawn to the rafters. His usually vibrant eyes had lost their gleam. His usually strong face had sunken on his skull. He looked like he'd lost his soul. Gichi took the small red box out of her pocket and held it out to him.

He hesitated before taking it, as if he feared it might singe his hand. But he took it, opened it, and held up the brass necklace. "Gichi, tell me the truth. How did you get this? Did you go out and retrieve it off the lake?"

She shrugged.

"And did you see me throw it out there last night?"

She shrugged again.

"Lass, don't go out in the middle of the night like that. Especially not during a snowstorm. Promise me you won't do that again."

She nodded, hoping it wasn't a lie.

He'd figured out that she saw him outdoors but asked no more questions, clearly having no idea she'd heard him inside talking to Miss Wright. Gichi felt relieved.

"I worked hard to save the money for this," he co
Schmidt has a few things like this from when he v
Because we are friends, he gave me a very good price ᴜ
couldn't afford to have words put on it and I'm glad for that. There
would have been no need to have Rebecca's name on it."

He replaced the necklace in the box, closed the lid, and held it for
so long Gichi thought he might give it back to her. But he put it in his
pocket.

"Let's go back to the house. I need to get cleaned up. Don't you
agree?"

She couldn't suppress one of her silent giggles, even though this
had been such a solemn conversation.

He started to get up but stopped, holding out a palm to implore
her to stay seated. "Gichi, I have a question for you. Do you think of
me as Mr. McIntyre or as Niall? I know children are taught to call
their elders by their title and last name. But I've been thinking about
this. Seeing that I think of you like a little sister, I hope you think of
me like a big brother. I hope you think of me as Niall and not as
stuffy, old Mr. McIntyre. So which is it? Do you call me Niall in that
pretty little head of yours?"

She didn't respond.

"Ah, I see. I'm Mr. McIntyre. Well, think about what I said and see
if you can find it in your heart to think of me as an older brother, not
as a stuffy, old grownup. Will you do that for me?"

She shrugged. She couldn't promise that would be possible.

He patted her head as was his habit, a habit she adored, and they
got up to go. He carried the tray and they returned to the warm
kitchen where Mr. Sterling had built up the fire to the point of feeling
like summertime. The light of dawn shone through the windows, and
Gichi knew that Mr. McIntyre's broken heart would mend after all.
Maybe not today, but surely before the summer solstice.

It would mend because he was loved by his friends on Mackinac
Island and his family back in Eire. A person couldn't have a broken
heart forever if they were loved. Could they?

She pondered that as she went about her day.

10

JUNE 22, 2022

"Are you enjoying your stay on the island?" Alexandra Ames asked.

"Oh, yes. We arrived only yesterday. They've never been here before ..." Wanda pointed at her friends "... and I haven't been since I was a kid. It's been great fun. We rode bikes this morning and made cairns on the beach. Then we had lunch at the Pink Pony."

"It's such a beautiful place. And so much history," Gale popped up. "I can't wait to tour the fort tomorrow."

"I love it here," Dawn added. "The yachts at the marina! I could walk around there all day hopin' somebody invites me for a ride."

Their host chuckled. "Yes, it is beautiful. I was born and raised here, right in this house in fact, and still spend five months a year here."

The four of them sat at the genealogist's kitchen table at her house that truly was "cottage" sized, unlike the mansions in town and on the bluffs that called themselves cottages. She'd given Wanda directions on the phone to come to her home in "the village", but there was nothing labeled "village" on the map they picked up at the Visitor's Center. However, by following Alexandra's street-by-street instructions, they landed in what the map called Harrisonville and came right to her door. So Harrisonville, they deduced, was called "the village" by the locals.

"I see you rode your bikes up here." Alexandra tittered. "Tough ride, isn't it? Especially on those old-time bikes. I should've warned you it'd be uphill."

"Yeah, we had to walk them most of the way," Wanda admitted.

"The good news is that it's all down going back."

Wanda loved Alexandra's good nature. She'd already made them feel at home by offering coffee or tea – they opted for coffee – and suggested they go by first names. She looked to be in her eighties, a healthy, vibrant octogenarian. Wanda adored her long, gray hair pulled up into a bun at the top of her head, stray ends boinging out to form a halo. She wore a colorful summer dress and sandals. Not the media's stereotype of an older woman. According to her website, her life had been anything but dull. As an archaeology college professor, she'd worked at digs around the world. She'd been born and raised on the island but spent her professional life at the University of Florida. Genealogy had become her passion in retirement. Consequently, she'd hardly retired at all.

"Now," Alexandra said, "what do you know so far about your possible family connection to the island?"

"Not a lot. But I do have a couple of clues." Wanda pulled out the aged family Bible from the tote bag she'd placed on the table beside her. She'd wrapped the frail book in a pillowcase to protect it, and when she took it out of the case Alexandra's eyes lit up. Wanda slid it over to her.

"Oh my. This is a real treasure." The historian's penchant for thoroughness showed as she examined the cover, front and back. Cautiously, she opened it up and inhaled audibly upon coming to the pages that documented births, marriages, and deaths. "Oh, what a glorious find. The first thing I notice is that this is a Catholic Bible. They're different from Protestant Bibles. They have the same 27 books in the New Testament, but this has 46 books in the Old Testament compared to 39. Ah ha, I see here that the first entry is a marriage in 1829, a Geneviève and Harold Smith. Well, that last name doesn't help much. And it doesn't list anywhere here where any of these people lived. If they were from here, maybe I'll find them in Saint Anne's records. The church is the best source for finding more information, although there were a few years when there was no priest, so the records are sketchy. Still, I can usually find something of value there."

"Well, here's the connection to the island." Wanda took the tattered, red, jewelry box out of her tote bag and opened it up. "Go ahead and look at the engraving on the back. It says 'Mackinac Island 1822'."

Now Alexandra's archaeological skills reigned as she gently lifted the piece of jewelry out of its box and examined it. "The inscription is rather crude, as if the jeweler either wasn't very good or didn't have the proper tools. It's a bit crudely made, as well, which indicates it's older than the Victorian era, although it's close in design. But during that era jewelry became much more refined. Gaudy still, for sure, but better made." She hit the button to pop it open.

"The names are Gichi and one we can't read," Wanda noted.

"Hmmm. That predates the Bible entries, but they were found together?"

"Yes."

"Then there's a good chance they're connected. Gichi might be the mother of Geneviève or Harold Smith. Hmmm, let's see." She took a magnifying glass off a shelf behind her and examined the inscriptions. "It says 'To Gichi, from Niall'."

"Really? Wow. We couldn't see that."

Alexandra nodded. "Gichi sounds Native. Niall is most likely Irish or Scottish."

"That's what the docent at the museum where we found these thought, too, about Gichi."

"I see the last entry in the Bible is, let's see, 1900. That's a good bit of lineage to make my job easier. Can you leave these with me until tomorrow? I have an opening at two. Maybe I'll know more by then."

"Sure. Keep them."

"Okay. In the meantime, there are excellent resources about the history of the island in the library and at The Island Bookstore.

Browse around and see if you want any of it. You'll find out what life was like here once upon a time. Nothing like today with the big houses and tourists and cruise ships. Your Gichi and Niall would have been here before all that."

"Thanks. I'll do that." Wanda rummaged through her purse to pay in cash.

While Wanda collected her money, Gale asked, "What Native American tribe lived here before Europeans came? My DNA shows that I have a sliver of Native American heritage, too. I've been fascinated with tribal history ever since."

"None permanently. Or at least very few people stayed through the winter. The island was considered to be a sacred place where Anishinaabek clans met each summer to trade, worship their Great Spirit, socialize, and find mates for the young people of marrying age. There would be thousands of teepees and lodges lining the shore, long before the French started building permanent structures. Oh, how I would have loved to witness that. There was a 'law' that no one could marry within their extended family, so the match-making part of the gathering was important."

"Thank God it was in the days before reality TV," Dawn interjected. "Some sleazy producer would've made a splashy, insipid, degradin' show out of it."

"Ah huh, I imagine so," Alexandra agreed. "It was all quite honorable. That's why it's hard to pin down what tribe someone came from, there was so much intermarrying. 'Anishinaabek' is what they called themselves. They were a large group of interrelated tribes that banned together to coexist quite peacefully most of the time. It was white men who gave them the tribal names we're familiar with, like Ojibwe, which is the French version of what the British later translated into Chippewa. Oh, forgive me. I could go on and on. But I have another appointment coming in a few minutes. He's a photojournalist and blogger who travels all over the world. He's waited for this meeting for so long, I don't want to keep him waiting for one minute."

Wanda's internal antennae buzzed. Could it possibly be that Mr. McIntyre? What were the odds?

One hundred percent, as it turned out.

Gale was the first out the door and Wanda heard her say, "Well, hello there. I believe we saw you at the dock when we came in. I'm Gale."

"Hello, Gale. I'm James."

Dawn stepped out and said, "Oh, hi. How's it goin', James? I'm Dawn."

Wanda quickly paid Alexandra with cash and went out to find the man – THE man – standing there. A shiver ran up her spine as she wondered if he was stalking them at the same time her skin sizzled with excitement. She told herself to calm the hell down.

"Hello, ladies. It's going fine. It's a pleasure to see you – again." Even though his words addressed them all, his eyes landed on Wanda.

"This is our friend Wanda," Dawn offered. "Wanda, dear, this is James. Say 'hello', Wanda."

"Hi."

"Hello, Wanda."

Good lord. His smooth, rich, baritone voice went down like fine whiskey. Wanda's skin alit with fire. She cleared her throat knowing she needed to say something else, but no more words came to her. She'd forgotten every one of them she'd ever known.

Her buddies saved the day by regaling him with how great Alexandra was and how much he'd enjoy meeting with her. The genealogist came to the door and invited him in. He bid the three friends goodbye and disappeared before Wanda could recover.

"Holy moly, why didn't you talk to him?" Dawn was aghast. "He's gorgeous."

"And he seems awfully nice," Gale put in. "You should give him a chance. I can tell he likes you. He stared at you the whole time."

"I, well, I didn't know what to say." The truth rolled off Wanda's tongue, leaving a sour taste in her mouth.

"Bless your heart. We're gonna have to teach you how to talk to a man."

"I talked to Ralph for twenty-five years."

"That dufus doesn't count." Gale shook her head in disdain. "This is a real man."

"Don't you worry, honey. We'll take care of your sweet little ass. We'll start with how to say somethin' besides 'hi' when a man talks to you. You know, kindergarten relationship tips."

"Yeah, and I've been wanting to say this for a long time." Gale shook her head. "We've talked about it before, and you wouldn't do it because Ralphy-Malphy didn't want you to. But you need to wear a touch more makeup. You're so pretty. It would enhance your beautiful features."

"Well, seein' that we're gettin' down and dirty here, that plaid blouse you have on – it makes you look like a tablecloth for a picnic table. Or maybe it would make a skirt for a Christmas tree. Whatever, it shouldn't be on that nice body of yours. I've been meanin' to tell you it needs to go into your Goodwill bag. Pronto."

Wanda had no choice but to listen to fashion and makeup tips as they climbed on their bikes and coasted down the hill to town.

11

DECEMBER 22, 1822

Gichi and Niall stared up at the Christmas tree that stood in the middle of their town. It had miraculously withstood the test of its first blizzard and looked pretty with its bows laden with snow.

Nary so much as a wisp of breeze blew to disturb it. Early morning sunlight prismed through the branches to give it a gossamer pink glow.

Gichi found it to be fascinating, it was so lovely. Perhaps that was its meaning after all, simply offering a gift of beauty to all who looked at it.

She found it impossible to tell what Niall thought. He looked awfully rugged after his heartbreaking night. Downtrodden. Tired. Paler than ever, even for a white man. Most surprising, he hadn't said anything.

A small crowd gathered to consider the tree, most in wonder but some in quandary and one or two in disapproval. Old Chief Joe, a Potawatomi, shook his head.

"Niall, did you remember to pray to the Great Spirit to honor the living thing that you killed?"

"No, Chief. I'm sorry. I didn't know I needed to do that."

"Yes. You can kill an animal for food and for its warm fur. You can kill a tree for shelter and for fire. Always, after you do, you pray to honor it for helping a human survive. But cutting down a tree only to make it stand up again? I'm not sure about that. I think you must pray for forgiveness."

Niall looked the blue spruce tree up and down, nodded, and put his hands up in prayer. "Chief Joe, seeing that I don't know how to do it, would you help me say this prayer?"

The chief spread his arms out wide and chanted in his native tongue while others held their hands in prayer or simply stood still in respect. Most inhabitants of the island, Indian and white alike, were Catholic. But whether coming from Anishinaabek ancestors or from merely living amongst the Indians, many respected the ancient native beliefs. They had long ago bonded with the natives in order to conduct fur trading business; they had married into their families; they weren't about to cause disruption to the profitable alliances that had been built over the years.

Prayer concluded, Chief Joe proclaimed, "Amen!" Niall and some of the others echoed his call.

"Thank you, Chief," Niall said as the crowd broke up. "I'm sorry if I was disrespectful. I've been a Catholic all my life and we don't think of those kinds of things. My ancestors would have. According to the stories passed down to us, they felt they were one with the earth."

"We feel the same."

Gichi looked from Niall to Chief Joe. She liked being in the presence of these two men. She'd known the old Indian all her life. His face was covered in interesting lines; his hair fell in a long white braid down his back; his deep voice resonated with calmness. He always smiled at her, as he did now. He put a hand on her head and even through her thick cap she felt the energy of his blessing as it passed into her body, a tingling sensation that wiggled down from the top of her head to the very tips of her toes.

He removed his hand and looked up at the much taller Irishman. "Indians have no problem joining our traditional beliefs with the Christian religion that was brought to us generations ago by the

French fathers. Some have forgotten our ancestors' ways but many like myself, and I hope like Gichi ..." he smiled at her again "... have not. We once believed in many different entities, but with one Great Spirit in the Sky above all others. So we can be Catholic and Indians, as both believe in an all-powerful One who created this earth."

"That sounds like Eire. Our ancestors believed in many gods and goddesses, but with one God of the Earth, Dagda. I believe that the Irish and the Indians are much alike."

"Yes. It seems we are brothers and sisters."

The three of them had started to walk toward Madame La Framboise's house, with the chief's lodge on the way. As they neared his home, he invited them in to sit by the fire and drink hot tea.

Once inside, they met the Chief's wife, Abedaubun, who greeted them warmly. The three who'd come in from the cold sat cross-legged by the fire in the center of the small birchbark lodge, and Abedaubun served them hot blackberry tea in fancy china teacups on saucers. Then she settled in beside her husband, her own steaming cup in hand.

Gichi had been a guest in this lodge several times, usually with Mother or Madame. She loved the smell of the fire, furs, and birchbark wood. This felt more like living near the out-of-doors than Madame's grand house, although she liked that, too.

Chief Joe casually sipped his tea. Satisfied, he asked Niall if he knew the story of the Mackinac Island Indians and their beliefs about the islands.

"Aye," Niall said, "I know a bit from the fur traders and from Madame. But I'm Irish, which means I love nothing more than a good story, no matter how many times I've heard it. We believe that telling a story once is shameless. It must be told time and time over, making it a little better each time."

The chief chuckled. "Again, the Irish and the Anishinaabek seem to be related. A love of storytelling. Believing in the same religion after having our old ways changed by missionaries generations ago. We both come from clans, families that are the center of our lives.

And I've been by the fires on the beach to know we both would never turn down an offer of whiskey."

Now Niall chuckled. "Nay, we would not. That would be rude, would it not? It does seem like we are of the same world."

"Perhaps, then, this story will sound familiar to you. Perhaps the Irish have similar stories. Did you understand what I meant when I said 'Anishinaabek'?"

"Aye. Madame has explained that many of the Indian clans here come from the same large family but are divided up into smaller groups."

"That is correct. Groups like the Odawa, Ojibwe, and Potawatomi. Of course, Madame would know, being a Métis with an Odawa mother. She was raised in her mother's village on the mainland before marrying Joseph La Framboise. Her mother and sisters were also Métis, of course, and ran fur trade businesses on the south shore."

Gichi knew that "south shore" meant the big land across the lake to the south. Her mind wandered as she thought about how she'd gone with Madame several times to both the south and north shores to pick up supplies. But Madame had never invited her to get out of the canoe. She'd never set foot on land in either direction, her feet having never touched any earth except that on her island. Her attention came back to the conversation as the chief asked another question of Mr. McIntyre.

"Do you understand what 'Métis' means?"

"I believe it's someone with an Indian parent and a French parent. Most often an Indian mother and a French father. It's a French word, correct?"

"Yes. There are many such people here now. It has become tradition for fur traders to marry into a tribe to seal a promise of doing business together. The tribesmen gather furs and the traders give them goods – things we never needed before but have now come to believe we must have. Cooking pots, plates, cups ..." he raised his flowery china teacup to prove his point "... utensils, cloth, wool, beads, blankets, weapons, and whiskey."

"Ah, there we are different," Niall said. "We had no equal trade, because after our clans' lands were stolen away by the British, we had nothing left to give but our souls. But that's a story for another time. Tell me, Chief, do you resent what the white people have done to your people?"

"No, my son. Such a feeling would do nothing. Our lives are all we have; we must not waste time wishing they were otherwise. I love our Lord God. I understand the fur trading business. I see many good people around me. I live on the most beautiful island on earth, surrounded by waters that provide more food than we can eat. I am not complaining, simply explaining what has happened."

Niall nodded understanding, then sipped his tea.

The chief went on with his story. "White people say Frenchmen were the first white people from across the big ocean to come here. Jesuit priests and fur traders. But the Anishinaabek and other tribes, the Huron and Iroquois, tell stories that have been passed down for generations, stories that say other white people were here long before that. Because we have no books, white people don't believe that. We believe our ancestors more than we believe white men's books."

Gichi liked this story, which she'd heard many times before. The chief's soothing voice lulled her into sleepiness, however, her eyelids heavy with a desire to close. After all, she'd been awake most of the night, worried about her friend who was now safely by her side. Her head bobbed and eased its way onto Niall's arm, like it sometimes did with her mother during mass on Sundays.

The next thing Gichi knew she was being carried outside in the cold, carefully held in strong arms. Her eyes opened enough to see the bottom of Mr. McIntyre's broad chin with its winter whiskers. Her first instinct was to pull on his coat to let him know she was awake. But a second impulse told her to let him carry her home. She squeezed her eyes closed tight and let herself melt into his brawny embrace. She loved the feel of him, the smell of him, the strength of him. It felt like .... Well, she had to think about that. Then she knew.

It felt like to having a big brother who loved her.

12

JUNE 23, 2022

"You know I'd never let you do this to me if I didn't consider you to be like a sister."

"I know, darlin'. Now stop pussy footin' around. You don't even need to try it on. It'll fit. Just take it to the checkout counter. Oh, here's another one." Dawn pulled out another blouse from the rack. The three of them were in a chi-chi women's shop in the main shopping district.

"I appreciate this, but I can't afford two. Or one, really. I'm living off a paltry alimony. Remember?"

Her companions knew well her horrifying story about discovering that all the bank accounts she and Ralph had were gone. They had still been married when she couldn't buy groceries one day because her charge card was rejected. A call to the bank resulted in the revelation that he'd ransacked all their accounts. When confronted, he insisted it was a stupid mistake. With Gale and Dawn's social media skills, however, they discovered he had a pregnant girlfriend, now his wife, right in Atlanta. Sharing that revelation with their beloved Wanda had been the most heartbreaking, gutwrenching experience imaginable.

"Oh, honey, I'm buyin' these," Dawn insisted.

"No. Absolutely not. No way. Uh uh."

"Way," Gale said as she came up behind them with a blouse of her own in hand. "And we're paying for your room, too."

"No."

"Yes. No argument. I've sold two houses since we've been here. Well, my assistant did. I didn't work all those years to build my real estate business not to spend my money. You deserve this. We're doing it."

"Besides," Dawn drawled, "it hurts my eyes to see some of the things you wear. You have a great body. Show it off, for the sake of the country."

Wanda scoffed at the blouse Dawn held up to show her. "Good lord, my cleavage will spill out all over the place."

"I know. Ain't it great? You've got it, so why not flaunt it?" Dawn shook her own ample bosoms to emphasize her point.

"If I recall," Gale reminisced, "it was Ralph who didn't want you to look too sexy. He was jealous. Am I right?"

"Well, yes," Wanda admitted.

"So to hell with knuckle-dragging scumbag Ralphy-boy. Forget him and be Wanda instead."

Wanda couldn't help but chuckle at the thought.

Dawn and Gale trotted to the counter with Wanda lagging behind. She'd never be able to afford to repay them in the same way. She'd have to think of something else. What that might be, she had no idea.

Her two friends chipped in to split the cost of Wanda's two tops, then each paid for one for herself. As they started to leave, however, Dawn turned to give the store a critical once-over.

"Excuse me, honey," she sweetly addressed the clerk. "Are you the owner?"

"Why yes."

"My name's Dawn and I'm a fashion retail store consultant. Have y'all ever considered rearrangin' your store a bit for wider appeal and better function? Look over here – if you moved this rack …"

Gale grabbed Wanda's arm and led her outside. "Let's leave her in peace to do her thing. She'll have a new client inside fifteen minutes. They watched through the window as Dawn pointed here and there and the owner nodded. Fourteen minutes later Dawn came out and announced that she'd be working in the store the next day.

"Now," she said to Wanda, "don't you feel better? You brought me here, which gave me a new client. Those new blouses and your room are your share of my take."

Wanda did indeed feel better.

It had been a good day. They'd had a casual breakfast at the inn and then toured the fort, which they totally enjoyed. Then they wandered down into the little town to shop, hitting the dress store first.

"I'm starved. I say it's lunchtime." Wanda pointed down the sidewalk where a plethora of eating places awaited.

They tumbled into Horn's Gaslight Bar and Restaurant, picking a booth that would accommodate them as well as their shopping bags. Lunch hit the spot and then, as was tradition on the island, they stopped at one of the many fudge shops for dessert.

Next came a visit to the Island Bookstore where they bought books they agreed they'd share. Avid readers all, they'd spent many an hour over iced tea discussing plots, heroes and heroines, romance scenes, and whether a book would make a good movie. If it would, the conversation turned to who would star in it.

Those conversations usually ended up with the same conclusions.

"I think Brad Pitt should star in that one," Dawn would say.

"You think Brad Pitt should star in everything," Wanda or Gale would retort.

"I know. That's because he should." Dawn would sigh.

"I think George Clooney should star," Gale would declare.

"You always say George Clooney," Wanda or Dawn would remind her.

"I know. I'm like Dawn. I think my guy should star in everything."

"I think Colin Firth would be good," Wanda would put in her two cents'. "Or Denzel Washington. Or maybe Daniel Dae Kim. Good lord he's gorgeous. Or for an edge they could do Johnny Depp."

"Darlin', you pretty much like every male actor who's ever done a kissin' scene."

It would be Wanda's turn to heave a heavy sigh. "I know. I guess when you're married to Ralph that's what happens."

On this day at the Island Bookstore, Wanda bought three books recommended by the staff about the history of the island. She had a pile on the counter with *Mackinac: An Island Famous in These Regions* on top and couldn't wait to dig into it.

"Look-ee here at what I found." Dawn brought her own stack to the counter. "Sweet second-chance romances." *Lilac Island,* a novella with a pretty purple cover, sat on top.

Gale appeared with two books. "Look at this one. It looks great." She held up *Dockporter* and the clerk told her it had been very popular. "In honor of Sean who took such good care of us."

Her friends had a hard time getting Wanda out of there. She wanted to sit right down on the floor and read all day. But she had another appointment with Alexandra, which she looked forward to, so pulled herself away.

Back in her room at the inn, she put on one of her new blouses, looked in the mirror, pulled on each breast to fluff it up, and laughed. The blouse, form fitting on top and flaring to the waist, looked great with her crop jeans and sandals. And yes, there was her ample cleavage for all the world to see. She'd even put on a little more makeup than usual and looked quite fetching if she said so herself. She threw on her sunhat and sunglasses, grabbed her purse, and headed downstairs.

There she discovered that both of her businesswomen friends were tied up with work calls, so she rode her bike by herself to her appointment with Alexandra.

"Oh, wait until you hear what I've found!" Alexandra greeted her without preamble. "Come, come. Sit down." She went straight into her kitchen and gestured to the chair at the table where Wanda had sat in the day before. "Let me show you."

"What? I can't wait."

They sat down, with the elder woman wiggling her butt in her seat, she was so excited. She opened Wanda's family Bible that she already had at hand.

"See this first couple?" She pointed to the first record of a marriage, Geneviève and Harold Smith in 1829. "There was no priest at Saint Anne's at that time, as I mentioned before, so their marriage wouldn't have taken place there. But I did find a Private Harold Smith stationed at the fort in 1830. And guess what! He is listed as married with a wife named Geneviève and an infant named Cassandra. Cassandra is the second marriage in your Bible, sixteen years later. Look at that." She tapped on the names. "So, I realized they fell into the timeframe when there was no priest and it was common practice for native women and white men to simply do some kind of informal civil ceremony and go about their married lives until a priest arrived to do a formal rite. That's what Madame La Framboise did, and she became very well known and respected. Do you know about her?"

"Yes. We're staying at the Harbor View Inn, her home. They have booklets about her. I was fascinated by her story. She and her husband were together for ten years before a priest solemnized their marriage vows."

"That's right. So your ancestors did the same thing but only for one year, as it turns out. Saint Anne's got a priest again in 1830 – they hadn't had one since 1765. Madame La Framboise and others ran Sunday mass in the log church she'd had brought to her land. The big, beautiful church that's there now was built later. So, Harold and Geneviève formalized their marriage at the little log church in 1830. Consequently, they wrote 1829 in the Bible for their common-law marriage, although the church records say 1830. Whew. Took me a bit to figure that one out. But that kind of thing happens all the time in this business. It's like being a detective investigating dead people. I love it."

"It's fascinating. That brings me closer to finding out about the rest of them."

Alexandra got up and without asking poured them each a cup of coffee. She came back to the table, and Wanda was grateful for something to drink after her bike ride up here.

"Oh, there's more," Alexandra said after taking a couple of sips of her brew. "Harold Smith is listed as being buried at the Fort Mackinac Post Cemetery in 1830. They were only together for two years. Sad. I don't know how he died. However, there were epidemics of influenza and cholera spreading around the country at that time, so disease is a possibility. There weren't any battles that year, so I doubt he died that way."

"Huh. We toured the fort this morning. I had no idea I had a connection to the place."

"You learned, then, about how the French first occupied the island. When a peace treaty was signed at the end of the French and Indian War in 1763, the Seven Years War some call it, Britain gained control of land east of the Mississippi, including the island. The French had built Fort Michilimackinac on the mainland. The Brits moved the fort here to the island. Then the United States got it after winning the Revolution, then the Brits took it back during the War of 1812. Then when the States won that war, we got it back." She slapped the table. "What a history!"

"We learned all about it, but it's hard to keep it straight."

"Well, imagine living through it. There's always been a rumor – mind you my academic mind shouldn't be participating in rumors, but this one is juicy – a rumor that during the War of 1812 when the Brits came, the American soldiers had to evacuate quickly, leaving behind some of the women and children. Well, two years later when the Brits had to leave and the Americans came back, there were a couple of wives who weren't all too happy about their American husbands' return. They liked the Brits better." Alexandra chuckled merrily. "Heavens to Murgatroyd, I love this business of digging into the past."

Wanda laughed with her, shaking her head.

"Anyway, I digress. Your family member's grave is out there at the Post Cemetery." She pointed in its direction. "You can go see it, if you want."

"I think I'll ride over there from here. Thanks. That's great."

"Well, unfortunately, after Cassandra, Geneviève and Harold's daughter, I lost track for a while. But in 1886 there's enough information here that I was able to find that couple and follow the line all the way to your great-grandparents. You have access to ancestry.com, right? Why don't you see what you can find, too. Between the two of us we should be able to cobble more of this together. Here, I've made a list of names and dates for you to add to your family tree." She handed a printed page to Wanda.

"Wow. This is fantastic. I had no idea you could do so much so soon. Is there anything about any of these people I need to know?"

"Not that I could find. By 1886 they'd moved off the island. There's a farmer's wife and a teacher, but most I don't know. I was only able to figure out where they lived. But at least that's a start."

Wanda used cash to pay the genealogist for all her hard work, and they agreed to meet again for a quick visit the next day. Alexandra's schedule was still packed.

Outside Wanda hopped on her bike and paused, one foot on the pedal and one on the ground. Should she go back to her lively friends or go visit the dead? Something deep inside her begged her to do the latter. She struck out to ride across the island to check out the Fort Mackinac Post Cemetery, the place of repose for one of the people who had made her.

13

DECEMBER 23, 1822

G ichi awoke to hear a flurry of activity in the kitchen. She got up, went to the door, and peeked out to see what was going on.

"And who is this person we're making all this fuss over? Getting up before dawn to bake new bread. Pfft. We have plenty of yesterday's bread left. But no. That isn't good enough for this stranger." Amelia whined as she took out her frustration on the bread dough she kneaded. "Besides, our big meal is supposed to be day after tomorrow, Christmas Day, in the name of our Lord Jesus Christ. Not today. It's too early. He isn't born yet."

"It's the new commander at the fort. He arrived yesterday. First Lieutenant Spencer's time here is over; he'll be leaving in the morning." Mother sliced beets as she chatted.

The warmth of the room drew Gichi in, and she padded in to put her back to the stealthy fire. Their sleeping room became frightfully cold during winter nights, "as cold as a witch's heart," her mother often said.

"There she be. Good morrow, my dove." Mother greeted her with a smile.

The girl nodded her greetings to Mother and Amelia.

"The new post commander." Amelia rolled her eyes in disgust as she ignored Gichi and returned to the conversation. "As if we don't have enough to do with Christmas coming."

"Oh, Amelia," Mother soothed, "you know it's always this way. The new commander is supposed to take his post at the start of the new year." She went to the fire and Gichi stepped aside so she could stir a kettle that hung over the flames. "But that's a dangerous time for the ice. If he waits much longer it will be solid and a boat won't get through. But it won't be solid enough to travel on until after his post starts. He has to come now or he'll be late for the start of his new post."

"Well," Amelia groused, punching the dough like a prize fighter, "I don't understand why anyone has to come at all. Our people have lived through French, British, Americans, then British again, and now Americans again. Why can't they all go away and leave us alone?"

"Amelia, we must accept the fact that is not going to happen." Mother turned her attention away from her grouchy helpmate and ran a palm over Gichi's head to tamp down her messy long hair. The girl used both hands to push wayward strands behind her ears, and Mother gently stroked her cheek. "Go get dressed and by the time you come back there will be nice hot porridge for breakfast." She pointed at the kettle.

Gichi wasted no time changing her clothes and getting back to the table for a hearty bowl of porridge covered in milk Mr. Sterling brought in fresh from the cow and topped with a few drops of the maple syrup they'd made themselves in the fall. Everyone got up out of bed and sat down to eat at the kitchen table, including Mr. McIntyre and Madame La Framboise.

After breakfast Gichi and Mr. McIntyre walked the few blocks to town to check on the Christmas tree. The snow had packed down and their snowshoes made it an easy walk.

The tree looked as pretty as ever, although different with much of the snow having fallen off its boughs and Mr. Schmidt's tin stars scattered about. Others had gathered to see it, too, and everyone seemed pleased to see it still standing, as if it represented an omen of good things to come.

Gichi thought it a perfect way to start the day before Christmas Eve.

Unfortunately, the day would be shattered before it was over.

Captain Fanning, the new post commander, was a nice enough man. He wore his uniform. His wife seemed pleasant. She wore a simple dress with a white lace collar. Madame explained to them that because they were having their Christmas meal early to accommodate them, her staff would be joining them. The Fannings were amenable, and the evening went by quickly. They ate in the dining room on the "good" china. Mother and Amelia had made a delicious meal – roast pheasant with beets and potatoes, buns with butter, and rice pudding for dessert. The adults even drank elderberry wine the guests brought with them.

But after dessert the captain asked Mr. McIntyre to join him for a cigar and tip of whiskey in the parlor. They retreated to the parlor and Gichi heard the doors close behind them.

Mr. Sterling excused himself to do his nightly chores in the stables.

The women chatted as they sat at the table, their attention rapt as Mrs. Fanning explained the latest fashion out of New York City: lower waistbands, poofy sleeves, and bigger skirts. She'd seen it recently when they traveled through the city.

Gichi couldn't imagine why anyone cared about the silly clothes American women wore in a place that was so far away. Besides, she itched to know what was going on in the parlor.

No one noticed when she morphed her body into a flexible fish that slunk out of her chair and stole away. Out of sight in the hallway, which was dim because the candles in the sconces had burned low as the evening went on, she put an ear to the parlor door. After all, Madame herself had taught her to do so when they eavesdropped on Mr. McIntyre and Miss Wright.

"This cigar is divine," she heard Mr. McIntyre say.

"It's from Cuba. It was given to me by an officer who had traveled through Boston, where boxes of these had recently come in at the dock. They're delightful, aren't they?"

Gichi could imagine the men puffing on the fat, brown sticks of tobacco. She'd seen cigars before and liked their smell. She wanted to try one someday.

Mr. McIntyre said something she couldn't hear. He must have turned away. Then she heard, "The whiskey is divine, as well. Thank you, sir."

"It is my pleasure. Now, the reason for this private meeting is that I have a letter for you." The commander paused, presumably while pulling the letter out of his pocket. "It arrived in Boston three months ago, made its way to Detroit where it languished at the fort, and finally made its way into my hands. And yours. I pray it brings good tidings from your family. As you can see, it is from Ireland."

Silence followed for so long it took every bit of strength she possessed to keep Gichi from charging into the room like a wild wolverine.

Eventually, Captain Fanning said, "I will leave you to your thoughts, Mr. McIntyre. Let me know if there is anything I can do to help."

"Yes." The Irishman's voice sounded raw with emotion. "There is. I'll need to depart tomorrow on the boat with First Lieutenant Spencer. It's most likely the last boat to leave the island for the winter. Do you think it possible for me to join them?"

"Of course. I'll see to it."

The parlor doors opened and the captain strode out. Gichi cowered in a dark corner, unseen. He went back to the dining room to retrieve his wife so that they could take their leave. While she could hear him and his wife thanking their hostess and the cooks, she took the chance to peek around the door into the parlor.

Mr. McIntyre stood by the fireplace, its flames casting melancholy, wavy shadows across his face. He held the letter in his hand but didn't look at it. He stared at nothing, lost to this place. That letter undoubtedly said something terrible. He wadded it up and cast it into the fire where it ignited in a flare.

Gichi could hear the grownups start to move out of the dining room and into the hallway, so she quickly slid out the front door and scampered around the house to the kitchen door, where she entered unnoticed. Busying herself with cleaning, she looked innocent as a lamb when her mother came in. Bent over the wash basin, dutifully scrubbing a pot, the girl could feel Mother's eyes burrowing into her back.

"So," Mother said, "what did you hear at the parlor door?"

14

JUNE 23, 2022

Wanda felt like a spy. There he was at the Post Cemetery, of all places, so focused on his work he didn't know she'd come up behind him.

James McIntyre.

She stood on the road with her bike between her legs, letting herself enjoy ogling him as he stepped aside from his tripod to look at the scene firsthand then look back into the camera. He repeated the process several times before she decided what she had to do.

Quietly, she got off her bike and leaned it up against a tree. She took a deep breath, looked down at her body, and shrugged. "Towanda," she murmured to herself as she swept her hair behind her ears, licked her lips, and stood up nice and straight. She walked up behind him.

"Hello."

He jumped, yelped, and spun around like a scared cat. He stumbled and she reached out to steady him. As he caught his balance, he accidentally swiped the side of the tripod and fumbled to catch it before it toppled over.

Wanda fell into the fray, grabbing at the camera only to knock his arm off course. Miraculously, he caught the camera and lifted it off the tripod a moment before it noisily banged to the ground. Thankfully, neither of them fell on their ass.

"Oh. Oh." He juggled the camera, which wanted to lurch out of his hands. He managed to clutch it to his chest like a running back while Wanda attempted to pick up the tripod. She dropped it. He set the camera on a rock and tried to help with the tripod, but they bumped heads.

"Go ahead," she said, backing away. "I'm so sorry." Damn, she thought. Apologizing again. At least she caught herself, which was better than usual.

"No, no." He let go of the tripod, abandoning the thing and letting it clamor to the ground. "It's my own fault. I was concentrating so hard I didn't hear you."

"Well then, how about neither of us apologizes, seeing that we both think it's our fault."

"Good idea. Very good." He ran a hand through his hair. They both fell into a nervous chuckle. "Hi. Oh, that was stupid. How are you? Damn. Not much better. Um, it's good to see you. When you wouldn't talk to me last night I figured either you're married with a jealous husband, you hated me on sight, or I'm so terrifying you're afraid of me. No need to be afraid, I swear."

Wanda wanted to kiss him. Right then. Right there. Smack dab on the lips. A long, succulent kiss to show him how much she adored him for being flummoxed by her presence. It had been a very, very, very long time since a man had been out of sorts over being near her.

She laughed, long and hearty. "One, I used to have a jealous husband, but no more. Two, I did not hate you on sight. In fact, it was quite the opposite. And three, you are not terrifying – at all."

"Good. That's all good."

"I think it's time for us to sit down somewhere and have a chat. What do you think?"

"Sure. Sure." He looked around and motioned toward the solemn rows of graves with their white crosses. "Maybe this isn't the best place to get to know each other, though."

"No, probably not. But there's one thing I want to do before we leave. You see, Alexandra discovered that I have an ancestor buried here. Private Harold Smith."

"No kidding? Let me help you find him."

She could feel him calm down, like she found herself doing, as they walked around looking at the markers. Most had no name. But before long he said, "Here. Private Harold Smith."

She joined him as they stared at the white cross. When she pulled her phone out of her pocket to take a picture, he offered to take one with his camera, too. After a few shots, however, his camera turned to her. She smiled and he took several shots.

"Wanda, I'd like some shots of you over by the brick wall at Saint Anne's Cemetery. That would be a perfect backdrop." He looked up at the sky. "This late afternoon light is just right, too."

They walked the short distance to that cemetery, going past the town cemetery on the way, and she posed this way and that as James politely guided her moves to catch the light. After fifteen minutes, he proclaimed success. They headed back to the post cemetery to pick up his mangled tripod and her bike, then walked down into town, with Wanda walking her bike all the way. She didn't want to miss one moment of time with James.

"So you're a professional photographer?" she asked as they started out.

"No, not in a traditional sense. I'm an independent photojournalist. Three times a year I go to a different place for a month and take photographs. Then I go home to South Carolina and sort and edit my photos to post on social media for the next three months. Then I do it again. It's a dream come true. It's what I've wanted to do for a very long time. I've been doing it now for three years. How about you? What do you like to do?"

Wanda had to think about that. Should she lie, making up something exciting and exotic to impress him? A successful online entrepreneur. A writer of erotic romance novels. A secret government agent?

"Actually, James, I was a homemaker and mother for twenty-five years. Now my two children are grown and gone, and my husband is gone, too. So, other than that, I don't know what I like to do. I'm exploring. I love history. I love exploring ancestry. I love to travel."

A tour carriage with eight passengers drove by and the tourists waved at them. A few bikers followed close behind, struggling to make their way up the hill.

When it quieted down, James said, "We love the same things. I'm divorced, too, by the way. Three years ago. No children. That divorce was my kick in the butt to do what I'd always wanted to do."

It seemed rude but Wanda, beginning to think of herself as Towanda, had to ask. No use wasting her time on another deadbeat. "James, do you make a living doing that?"

He stopped and looked her over. She stopped and looked him over right back.

"You're a practical woman, Wanda. I like that. A lot. I'm a practical person myself and respect it in others. The truth is, no, I don't make much of a living at it. I do make something when I'm hired for a job like this. I love this island and have been here on my own so much and posted so many photos, the tourism bureau asked me to come and do it officially."

"So how do you live?"

He smiled broadly. "Quite well. You see, I worked very hard for a very long time to build up an internet company. After my divorce I sold it for enough to sustain me for, well, ever."

"Really? Forever. Gee. That's a lot." Doubt showed on her face.

"Yes, it is. Wanda, will you come to dinner with me? Let's make an evening of it?"

She shoved doubt aside and smiled. "Yes. I'd like that."

He walked her to her inn, where she left her bike. Calls to the girls' rooms netted no responses, so she left them texts telling them to have dinner without her. The two of them ambled into town, laughing along the way at the dorkiness of their meeting at the cemetery.

"We're both hopeless nerds," she said.

"Oh, I've known that about myself for a long time. But you? No way. You're nothing but beautiful."

"Why thank you, James."

She felt beautiful. And happy for the first time in years.

Over dinner she noticed some amazing differences between Ralph and James. James let her finish her sentences before speaking. Ralph always interrupted her, as if she were too stupid to know what she really wanted to say. James didn't one-up or "mansplain" anything she said. Ralph was a freaking master at that. And James's tone of voice with her, and with everyone including the restaurant staff, was smooth and respectful. Ralph often spoke with a note of disdain, especially to clerks and servers, people he considered to be beneath him in all his highfalutin glory.

It struck her that her parents would love this guy. Their relationship with Ralph had always been strained. Her father had always treated her mother the way James was treating her right now.

James made her realize how much she'd allowed herself to mold to and put up with Ralph's arrogant bullying. James also made her realize she'd never put up with that again.

When the conversation turned to their former marriages, James set the tone.

"My marriage ended when I discovered my wife was having an affair with the man who was supposed to be my best friend. Talk about a double kick in the ass. He was married, too. His wife was destroyed by the discovery. At first, I was too and really pissed off. But eventually I accepted it and walked away to start a new life. I refused to be dragged down by it. Besides, I didn't really see any other choice that would make me happy."

Wanda sipped her wine as she considered his brave handling of such a hellacious thing. She hadn't been so brave. At least not yet.

"My husband is an executive for an airline, and I discovered he had a girlfriend, now his pregnant wife, that he took with him on business trips. So there. How's that for a crappy marriage?"

"Whew. That's pretty crappy. Let's toast to bad breaks that led to our new beginnings."

They clanged glasses and looked at each other over the rims as they drank their wine. And Wanda knew she wanted to spend nights and days and weeks, and maybe even longer, with this man. It felt as if she'd been longing for James McIntyre all her life.

15

DECEMBER 24, 1822

Gichi didn't want Mr. McIntyre to go away. Yet here they were, everyone in the household, standing in the kitchen at daybreak on this cold Christmas Eve day, saying goodbye.

She'd hardly slept a wink, what with the sound on the ceiling of his footsteps pacing in his bedroom above, back and forth, back and forth, telling her he fretted over something terrible. When Madame called them out of bed and gathered everyone together, they hurriedly dressed and scurried into the kitchen in anticipation. They stood there listening – Gichi, Mother, Amelia, Mr. Sterling, and Madame – as they heard his heavy footfall, clop, clop, clop, come down the stairs. They were taken aback when he walked into the room. He looked terrible, as if he'd been wrestling with his heart and lost.

"Sit down. Everyone. Please," he pleaded. "This is going to be hard enough as it is. We may as well sit." They scrambled to the table. He placed his palms flat on the wood, as if to keep his hands from shaking. "As you know, me friends, the commander took me into the parlor last night for a private conversation. He had a letter for me from home. Me Da is very ill and not expected to live. At least, that's the way it was months ago when my sister sent the letter. I'm afraid I must go home. I'm the eldest son. It is my duty to make sure my family is taken care of."

"Oh, Niall," Madame moaned. "Are you sure you must leave? Is there anything else we can do?"

"No, I'm afraid not. I haven't been able to send back money as I'd hoped. You see, I had fanciful ideas about coming to America and getting rich. I'd heard about the Irish who came to this country. Some never made it past the poverty of cities like New York and Boston. They are called 'shanty Irish'. You probably know that." Everyone else at the table shook their head. They hadn't known that. "But others, those who work hard and are clever and lucky, which we Irish are supposed to be, make good money and move up in life. They're called 'lace curtain Irish.' I was determined to come here and make it good, and send me ma a set of lace curtains, like those that hang in the front parlor here."

Gichi caught a look that passed between Madame and Mother. She knew those curtains were about to come down.

"I'm a good fisherman," the Irishman went on. "I know that for a fact. I come from generations of fishermen in Galway. I imagined having a big business selling fish. I came to the island because I heard about the good fishing here. And it is. My ideas about a big company are good ideas. But they would take time. More time than I have. So, alas, I must take me leave from this family we have made ourselves here. I must go back to my birth family in Eire. But I will always love my family here, as I love those back home."

Tears streamed down every woman's face. Mr. Sterling blinked. Gichi sat there frozen as the lake in January.

"Niall," Madame said, "let's be practical. How do you intend to get back to Ireland?"

"I will work me way to one of the cities with boats that cross the ocean. I'm strong. I know the sea. I will find work on a ship that will take me home."

Madame frowned, causing a worry line to etch itself into her forehead.

"Gichi, me bonnie colleen," Mr. McIntyre said, "I have something for you."

Gichi thawed and leaned forward as he pulled the red box out of his pocket.

"I will tell the truth, little one. We all know that, unfortunately, I originally bought this for someone else. But fate played a trick on me and showed who really deserves this gift. This is for you, Gichi." He held the box out to her.

She looked at it, then looked back at him. He nodded. She took the box out of his hand and opened it. There, nestled in the red silk, lay the brass locket. She picked it up and ran a finger over the design on the front.

"Turn it over and let me tell you what it says."

Surprised, she turned it over to see writing on the back. She couldn't read, so didn't know what it said.

"It says, 'Christmas, 1822.' I want you to remember this Christmas with our tree in town. Now, let me show you how to open it." He clicked the tiny lever on the side, and it popped open. "This side," he said, pointing, "says 'Mackinac Island', so you'll always remember I was here. And this side says, 'To Gichi, Love Niall'. Remember what I told you about being your big brother and you could think of me as Niall?"

She nodded.

"That's why I put that name there instead of Mr. McIntyre. And because Mr. Schmidt couldn't fit it in."

That garnered grins on the long faces around the table.

"Here, dear, let me help you put it on." Her mother stood up and took the delicate necklace from her daughter. "Hold your hair." Gichi held her hair up out of the way while Mother clasped the locket behind her neck.

"I'm sure she's very grateful, Niall," Mother said. "Thank you so much."

"It's a beautiful gift, Niall," Madame added. "Give me a minute, please, while I get something I want to give to you. Amelia, will you help me? And the rest of you, please see to it that this man eats well before he goes."

Mother fixed eggs, bread, and jam and fed the traveler. Then she packed a satchel of food for him to take with him. Mr. Sterling left and came back with a pottery jug of milk for him to take. Gichi saw the older man slip a bottle of whiskey to Mr. McIntyre, too, who placed it in the satchel he'd brought down from his room, the one that held his meager wardrobe.

Madame and Amelia returned to the kitchen. Madame had the lace curtains from the parlor folded in their arms. "These are for your mother, Niall. Her American lace curtains. Please give them to her with my love. Thank her for loaning her son to us to be part of our family for a while."

She handed over the curtains and Niall held them as if they were a newborn babe. Seeing that he seemed incapable of moving, she took them and carefully placed them in his bag with his clothes. Only Gichi was able to see that Madame stuck an envelope into the folds of the curtains. The girl knew Madame well enough to know it contained money.

With misty eyes, their Irish friend said, "Thank you, Madame. I pray to see you all again someday."

With that Niall McIntyre grabbed his satchels and coat and fled through the kitchen door. Like a herd of buffalo, everyone followed him out, trudging through snow to get a glimpse of the last of him.

He ran like a buck in the woods.

Gichi watched his backside become smaller and smaller until it vanished.

He was gone! Her friend was gone!

She ran like a doe, ignoring the snow that soaked through her indoor moccasins and the freezing cold that seared into her uncloaked body. She ran to town and down the dock, arriving in time to see her friend get into a boat with Lieutenant Spencer and two oarsmen.

"Niall!" she screamed. "Niall! Don't go!"

All eyes turned to her in shock. Niall jumped out of the boat, squatted down to look her in the face, and took her by the shoulders.

"Gichi! Me love, you spoke. And you did it for me. For me, your big brother. Bless you, me bonnie colleen. You must speak more. You must speak your mind. You must never stop telling others what's in that brilliant head of yours. Promise me, Gichi. Promise me you will continue to speak."

Tears streaming down her face, she nodded.

One of the oarsmen hollered, "Niall, we have to go. The lake is freezing over fast as a spreading plague."

Niall kissed Gichi on the forehead, tapped her locket as a reminder, and got back in the boat. He took up an oar and paddled hard, not turning back to look at the island again as the boat fought its way through encroaching ice shards. Even though his back pulsated with the effort of arduous rowing, Gichi could see his shoulders quake with despair.

Mother appeared with her wrap and bundled her up. Mr. Sterling pulled up in the buckboard and insisted she ride home with him to keep her feet from freezing any more than they already were. Madame and Amelia were there, too, and the makeshift family watched until the boat carrying their friend became a mere speck on Lake Huron.

16

JUNE 24, 2022

They stood on the shore looking out over Lake Huron. The night was sultry and calm – to Wanda, sexy.

They'd had a long, delightful dinner. They chatted about their hopes and dreams, and Wanda confessed to wanting to work with something historical, maybe even ancestry. James listened intently, nodding with interest. His dream was to use his photojournalism to not only show people the world but to make them happy in the process. He adored running into what he called "new friends I haven't met yet". They talked about how much they loved to travel. And they discussed their mutual interest in their own ancestries and their visits with Alexandra.

James had put his arm around her waist as they left the restaurant and walked to the edge of the water. The feel of his touch, even through her spiffy new blouse, electrified her, as if a wellspring of secret, bottled-up longings had suddenly been released. When they reached the edge of the water, he dropped his arm from around her and they faced one another. He laid his hands on her shoulders. She rested her palms on his chest.

His eyes – one of the first things she'd ever noticed about him was what a vivid lake blue they were, inviting her to dive into his soul.

Without words, their bodies gravitated toward one another, their mouths moving closer and closer. Wanda let her lips part, ready …

"Wanda!"

The want-to-be lovers jerked apart and looked in the direction of the call that came from a frantic male voice.

Her knees gave out from underneath her; she crumbled into James's arms. He caught her and croaked, "What in hell?"

"What in the name of the devil are you doing here, you damned bastard?" Dawn appeared out of nowhere and whacked Ralph Woods with her prized American Darling purse.

"You freaking creep, go away!" Gale joined in the fray with a whop of her no-name thrift store bag.

Wanda's ex-husband shielded himself with raised arms, howling and swatting at his attackers.

"Ralph! What are you doing here?" Wanda's bones found their strength and she stood up on her own to confront her ex. "And how did you find me?"

"You texted the kids. They told me. I've been trying to get ahold of you for days, and I've been on this god-forsaken island out in the middle of nowhere for three hours looking for you. Listen, Wanda. Honey, you need to listen to me. Okay, just listen." Wanda marveled at his inability to round up a vocabulary.

All Gale did was take one step toward him, and he spastically swatted at her as if being swarmed by a deadly colony of stinging bees. She halted. He righted himself and focused on the couple in front of him.

"Who in hell is this?" he spluttered, jabbing a thumb at James.

"Mister, you don't need to be approaching your ex-wife in this rude manner." James defended Wanda, she noticed, rather than himself. She liked that.

"Who in hell are you to tell me what to do?" Ralph's chin jutted out obstinately; his jaw worked itself into a frenzy; his hands balled into fists; his face turned as red as a radish.

"Oh, good god, Ralph," Wanda groaned. "Get out of eighth grade.

This is my date. Not that it's any of your business. Now answer my question. What are you doing here?"

He threw her a look of utter disbelief. "I thought you didn't want a divorce."

"That was before I knew you'd been screwing around for, oh, let's see." She tapped her chin with a forefinger, feigning confusion. "We were married for twenty-five years. So I guess that would be, hmmm, twenty-five years. What on earth has brought about this change in you? Wait. You know what?" She held up her hands to stop him from answering. "Never mind. I don't give a rat's ass. We're divorced. It's over."

"Honey, sweetheart, not that I'd planned on announcing it to the whole damned world ..." he gestured angrily at her friends "... but my heart is bleeding. I miss you. I want you back. We can't go on like this."

Wanda studied her ex in all his pathetic wonder. He seemed shorter. And his eyes looked – what? – shallow, she decided. No diving into a soul he didn't have. She even saw his body in a new way. It looked – doughy. Not exactly the Pillsbury Dough Boy but too close for comfort.

Not to mention the glaring reality that he was a flaming reprobate.

"Marrying Ophelia was a mistake," he simpered. "I'm too old to be the father of twins. I don't want to do that."

"Oh, good grief." Gale let loose with one of her famous eye-and-head rolls. "You're going to be the father of twins whether you want to or not. Do you need a middle school sex ed refresher course?"

"How 'bout *Sex for Dummies*?" Dawn suggested, holding her purse at the ready.

"I don't appreciate all these references to immaturity," Ralph scoffed.

"And we don't appreciate you being an immature dipshit. Go away." Gale took two steps toward him, and he backed up.

"That's for Wanda to say, not you," he shook a finger at Dawn and

Gale. "You know, you two always have been against me. I blame you for putting a wedge between us."

"Nah, it wasn't a wedge on our part. It was your ..." Dawn volleyed, pointing a swirling finger at the part of his body in question.

"He's right," Wanda cut in. "It's for me to say. So Ralph, I'm saying it." She stepped up to him and with hands on hips leaned in to stare him down. "Go away. Our life together is over."

"No, Wanda, honey, it can't be."

She considered him for a moment – the man she'd given her all, the father of her children, the one she'd long thought she'd grow old with – and knew there was only one thing to do.

She turned on her heel to face James, who stood there looking like a prince in shining armor poised to save his damsel in distress. But he hadn't. Instead, he hadn't intruded while she saved herself.

She loved him for that.

Slowly, with determination in each step, she strode up to James, reached up to take his face in her hands, and pulled his head down to hers. The kiss was extraordinary, like a marriage of everything that ever was and ever could be. Lost in that kiss, she became consumed by an awakening in her body of sensations not lost but never discovered.

The rest of the world faded away, even the continued bickering between her friends and her furious ex-husband. That didn't matter. Nothing else mattered. Nothing else existed.

James wrapped his arms more and more tightly around her as their bodies melded together. The kiss deepened. Wanda let herself float away into a dream world of sheer bliss.

There would never be any going back. It was one of those times in life when one thing changed everything.

When they finally came up for air, they grinned at each other in mutual understanding. A bond had formed; a pact had been made. It had more to do with their hearts and souls, but their bodies were involved, too.

"Would you like to join me for a drink at the Grand's Cupola

Bar?" he asked. "There's a spectacular view from there. The night lights will be stunning."

She nodded. "That sounds wonderful."

Without so much as a glance back at the others – Wanda knew her forever friends would handle Ralphy-boy and the cocky jerk would be sorry he ever showed his face here – the fledgling lovers walked away from the shore, up a couple of side streets to Cadotte Avenue, and up the lovely tree-lined road to the iconic Victorian-era hotel where James was staying. There was pausing and kissing along the way.

When the hotel came into full view, Wanda was dazzled by the sight. She hadn't seen the truly grand place at night. The long stretch of four-story white exterior emitted an ethereal effervescent glow in the dark. Night lights on the longest porch in the world revealed guests relaxing in rocking chairs as they took in the view of the straits where Lakes Huron and Michigan met under the lighted Mackinac Bridge.

As they came to the steps that led up to the porch, James greeted the doorman by name and introduced Wanda to him. The man in his impressive red uniform nodded and tapped two fingers to his top hat. The gesture on the part of both men made her feel acknowledged and appreciated. Included, not an aside as she'd become accustomed to.

She mattered.

When they stepped inside, the interior of the hotel took her back in time, as she felt certain it did for everyone who crossed its threshold. They went up the stairs to the Cupola Bar, where they each ordered a glass of wine. They quickly discovered that neither was much of a drinker, so one glass apiece did it.

As they held hands across the table and gazed into each other's eyes, the shocking yet titillating reality of the situation sunk in. They were grownups. They were single. They could do whatever they wanted.

And that they did.

17

OCTOBER 25, 1830

He had never excited her. Kissing hadn't been necessary, as she sometimes heard her women friends talk about so passionately, because he never did it.

As Gichi stared into the grave of her dead husband, memories of the lackadaisical intimate occasions they'd shared rolled through her mind. The only way she'd made it through his bashing was to imagine someone else.

The first time it had been Niall, the kind, handsome Irishman who'd left the island eight years earlier and had never been heard from since. However, when she recalled the promise she'd made to him that she would marry for love, she decided it was best he had vanished. Surely, if he saw the state of her marriage, he'd be disappointed in her for breaking her promise. So she wiped him from her mind.

The heroes she read about in books took over when her husband had his way with her, a dashing Norman knight here, an adventurous Templar there, and chivalrous Robin Hood almost everywhere.

Was it strange for a new widow to think about her imaginary lovers while staring at her husband's coffin?

She supposed so.

But even though her marriage, especially her sex life, had been less than gratifying, she would never be sorry for marrying Private Harold Smith because she would never be sorry for having the daughter they made together. In fact, having a child had been her sole reason for wanting a husband. At age fifteen, an age when girls married, after all, she'd had an overwhelming longing to have a child and to be a mother like her own mother. When the private proposed, even though she barely knew him, she said yes against the objections of Mother and Madame. He wasn't Catholic, so they married in the custom of the country, in the Odawa way, which meant they made a pledge to each other and started living together. It had been as simple as that. She gave birth nine months later.

Cassandra cooed in her arms, the infant's mouth puckering and sucking on air. When no ripe nipple appeared, her little pink forehead wrinkled up like a prune and her fists rivaled those of a miniature boxer. Her cackle meant the bellow of an angry bear was about to let loose. Gichi unbuttoned her blouse – she'd relented and started wearing American clothes when she married – and positioned her bosom to satisfy her bébé. Cassandra suckled greedily, happy at last. When the infant finished, Gichi put the little one up to her shoulder as mothers had been doing since the beginning of time and patted her back.

At the very moment the priest made his final sign of the cross over the grave and declared "Amen", Cassandra belched like a drunken sailor. Spontaneous laughter erupted from the crowd of mourners.

Gichi's sentiments exactly.

Ceremony over, everyone lined up to take a handful of dirt from the mound piled by the grave and drop it onto the pinewood casket. There was Mother, Madame, Mr. Sterling, the latest post commander Lieutenant Clark and his wife, most of the soldiers, Chief Joe and his wife Abedauben, others from the island, Reverend and Mrs. Ferry, the doctor's wife Mrs. Beaumont, Gichi's girlhood friends from school, and the women friends she'd made while living at the post with her husband, Army wives like herself. She treasured her friends.

As people left the Post Cemetery, they complimented the new permanent priest, Dominican Black Friar Father Mazzuchelli, for such a touching requiem mass, and they murmured condolences to Gichi.

She didn't know what to say, which she'd struggled with the night before during Harold's wake, too. The truth was, although she would never have wished him dead, she wasn't going to miss her husband one bit. Before he died in a fall off a horse, she'd already decided that when he transferred to another post she wasn't going. She and Cassandra would stay on the island. She would continue to work in Madame's kitchen with her mother, which she'd been doing for four years ever since Amelia married a Polish man and moved to the north shore with him to set up a mill.

It was not unheard of for a Métis or Indian wife to stay with her native family if her French-Canadian or American spouse moved away. Some mixed marriages were happy; some were not. Gichi's was not.

"My love, let me take her." Mother reached out to take the sleeping child. "You've been holding her the whole time."

Gichi handed over her baby. Madame put a reassuring hand on Gichi's back but remained silent. The young widow felt grateful her godmother hadn't uttered empty platitudes. The women in the La Framboise household knew that, although there would be sadness and prayers for the death of a soul, there would be little mourning for the loss of the life of heartless Harold Smith, who'd turned out to be a cold brute of a man.

Mr. Sterling pulled up in the buckboard and hopped down to help Madame and Mother get in. He held out a hand for Gichi but she spied two of her best friends lingering nearby, waiting for a chance to talk to her.

"Go," her astute mother said. "Our little darling is sleeping like a lamb. She won't awaken for hours."

"Thank you, Mother. I won't be long." She waved goodbye as the wagon headed for home.

Alexsie and Josette hurried to her side. They were white, like most post wives, but Gichi's light tan skin had never bothered them.

"I have a new book for you," Alexsie announced. "My sister sent it to me. It's called *Frankenstein*, by a woman named Mary Shelley. Oh, Gichi, it's excellent. You'll love it. It's scary but sweet at the same time. I read the whole thing in two nights." She pulled the novel out of the satchel that hung from her shoulder and handed it over.

"Thank you. I can't wait to read it." Gichi took the volume and protectively held it to her chest with both hands.

"Here. Let me carry it. I'll give it back when we reach your house." Alexsie took the book and replaced it where she'd got it, not only so Gichi wouldn't have to carry it but so no one would see her with it. They read in secret as much as was possible.

The three of them were about the same age and one of the things that bound them together as friends was their mutual love of reading. They devoured as many novels as they could get their hands on in this remote island. Incoming Army wives and, surprisingly, a few visiting preachers' wives had turned out to be prolific suppliers. They'd even managed Shakepeare's *Roméo et Juliette* in French, which they'd discussed for hours. Another favorite, this one in English, was *Ivanhoe: A Romance*, all three volumes, by an unknown writer.

When Gichi was seven years old she made up her mind to learn to read the moment Niall McIntyre gave her a locket with writing on it. She even gave in and went to Mr. Ferry's mission school where she became a voracious reader. Although most of what they read there was religious, there was history, too, which she loved.

She also discovered that she loved to talk. She supposed she had Niall, the vanished Irishman, to thank for that.

"Oh but wait!" Josette excitedly skipped backwards and stopped in front of them. Gichi and Alexsie came to a halt like obedient soldiers. "Yesterday I got one from a woman who came in with her husband. I'll let you both read it when I'm done. I was up half the night. I couldn't stop. It's the most, well, shall I say 'intimate' thing I've ever read. Very naughty. Don't let your mothers know you have it."

"What's it called?" Gichi's interest peaked.

"*Don Juan* by a man named Lord Byron." Josette heaved a dreamy sigh. "'Lord Byron'. Can you imagine?"

They giggled. "No," Gichi and Alexsie said on top of each other.

Gichi felt such relief talking to her friends. They weren't any more interested in discussing dead Harold than she was.

The three young women trotted down the dirt road toward the town as they chatted. Wagons and other walkers leaving the cemetery passed by as they moseyed along, many waving as they went.

The fall day oozed with the smell of the change of season. Inland, where they were now, the sugar maple, beech, and oak trees had turned varying shades of crimson and gold, interspersed with white pines. Autumn was Gichi's favorite time of year. But she said that about every time of year. Around the rim of the island, where it was cooler and more damp, a fragrant forest of spruce, birch, and cedar trees awaited.

They ambled around a corner, speculating about this myste-rious Lord Byron as they went. Gichi had confided to no one except these best friends, as this wasn't a conversation to have with her mother or godmother and certainly not a priest at confession, that she dreamt of Niall McIntyre returning one day and marrying her. When she'd been a child, she'd fancied him her big brother. But now that she was a grown woman with a child of her own, she had grownup desires. It was often Niall's friendly face, along with the imaginary faces of her fictional heroes, she imagined when her husband disapproved of her, which was a daily occurence.

According to Harold, she spent too much time outdoors coddling animals and smelling wildflowers. She wasn't a good enough cook. She didn't darn his socks fast enough. She wasn't pretty enough. She read too many vile books.

"Perhaps," she told her friends, turning her mind away from her cruel husband, "this Lord Byron looks like Niall McIntyre." She tugged on the chain around her neck to pull the locket she always wore out from under her collar. She ran a thumb across the cool metal that never failed to give her comfort.

"He sounds so handsome from what you say," Alexsie swooned. "I wish I could have met him."

"I only saw him a few times and I wasn't interested yet in how a man looked. All I remember is the smell of fish." Josette crinkled her nose.

"He didn't always smell like fish," Gichi said. "Sometimes he smelled like, well, like my father."

They fell silent until rounding a curve in the road where they could see past the trees and on down to the shore.

"What's going on?" Gichi picked up the pace.

"Everybody's gathered at the dock instead of going home," Josette proclaimed.

"An unusual boat must be coming ashore or there wouldn't be such hubbub," Alexsie speculated.

Boats and canoes came and went all the time. This was different.

They trotted to the shore and Gichi angled her way through the crowd in time to see Niall McIntyre emerge from a large canoe and jump onto the dock.

He had come back. For her?

Her heart stopped. Her lungs froze. Her mind went blank.

She crumbled to the ground.

18

JUNE 25, 2022

"Well, hello stranger. Long time no see. Come on over here and talk to us." Gale playfully tapped her finger on the table to indicate to Wanda, who'd just come in, to join them.

Wanda nodded, held up a finger for "in a minute", and went to the breakfast bar where she fixed a giant plate of scrambled eggs, toast, and bacon and poured herself a mug of black coffee. She sat down, threw out a raspy "hi", and alternated between chowing down and gulping her morning brew. She wore the same clothes she'd had on the night before. Her makeup had since disintegrated. Her hair seemed to be entertaining the notion of housing a family of hawks.

"Ah, honey," Dawn droned, "you look like y'all either had the time of your life or y'all were mugged. Which was it? Or both?"

She and Gale guffawed together.

"Well," Gale said, "we know he didn't steal her virginity."

They laughed again.

"Come on. Spill. We want the skinny. Although, he isn't skinny. He's perfect." Dawn chortled. "And he wears good shoes. That's an added plus."

"So you figure you know he's okay because of his shoes?" Wanda teased her friend.

"Ah ha. He takes good care of them. That tells us he isn't a slob. That's very important."

They sat in the breakfast room at the inn where Dawn and Gale had finished their breakfast and sat sipping their coffee.

"We thought we might not see you all day." Gale grinned mischievously.

"Huh. I could use some sleep. But I have an appointment with Alexandra and James has a meeting with the group he's taking photos for. I need clean clothes."

"That goes without saying. Did he walk you back or hire a carriage or what?" Gale asked.

"Carriage." Wanda talked in-between bites of her toast with eggs piled on. She was famished. "It's taking him to his meeting right now."

"So-o-o? How did it go-o-o." Dawn glanced at Gale and they exchanged smirks.

"Oh, you two. It went great actually, once I got over the jitters about being with somebody who seems too good to be true. But I won't say one more word about that until you tell me what happened with Ralph. Thank you, by the way, for taking care of the scumbag for me."

"Oh, don't worry. We 'escorted' the creep to the dock. It was too late for him to catch a ferry, so he whined about what he was supposed to do for the night." Gale's impression of the man's petulant face amused Wanda. "As if we would ever help him out."

"I tried. I suggested that he die, rot, and go to hell," Dawn said, "but he didn't seem to find that helpful."

"We left him there on his phone trying to find a room. As far as we could tell, everything is booked and he was left out in the cold, so to speak."

"I can't believe he showed up here," Wanda mused. "We're so done there's nothing on earth that could salvage that marriage."

"Okay, enough about the rat." Dawn flipped a hand in dismissal. "We want to know how y'all got along in the rack with that buck."

"How do you know James and I hit the rack?"

"Oh please," Gale mocked. "We might be beautiful, and brilliant, and ..."

"And sexy as Marilyn in the flesh," Dawn added, nodding emphatically.

"Yes. But we ain't stupid."

Wanda wiped her hands on her napkin, pushed her empty plate away, and grinned. "It was ... magical. It isn't that I'd forgotten how good it could be. I never knew."

"Well, alrighty then!" Dawn slapped the table.

"Way to go!" Gale cheered.

"He's so ... so ..." Wanda struggled to find the right words "... so real. Unpretentious. Easy to be with. Attentive. Not to mention smart and interesting. And funny."

She and her best friends had never shared the down and dirty details of their sex lives. They were, in the end, rather conservative and their first loyalty was to their husbands. Wanda didn't go into details about how her night with James had quickly turned from tenderness to ravenous.

"Ah ha. Well, darlin', we have news for you," Dawn said as she pointed at Gale. "There's more."

"Yes. While Dawn was working at that shop yesterday and you were busy with your new 'friend', I did some digging on the internet. You won't believe what I found."

"Oh no. Is he married? He has twelve children, right? All by different women. Or he claims to be an alien from outer space. Or he's wanted for embezzlement. There's a warrant out for his arrest. He's an imposter. He scams women for all they've got. What?"

"Not even close. Get this." Gale read off her phone. "Forbes Magazine, January 2022. Mr. James McIntyre from Bluffton, South Carolina, a self-made multi-millionaire in the IT arena, comes from the world-renowned McIntyre family known for its yacht manufacturing empire, founded in Detroit, Michigan. James McIntyre chose to step out of the family business and carve his own path in the IT industry and has since sold that business to follow his dream of being a global photojournalist. With over 250,000 followers and counting on social media, he clearly makes a success of whatever he pursues."

Wanda blinked. "What? He's a 'multi-millionaire'? He said he sold his business and was set for life, but I thought that meant, like, living on a fixed income for years to come. Like being careful not to spend too much on dinner."

"Honey, eat all you want. It's a fixed income all right. Fixed really high," Dawn noted. "According to what she found, he still has an interest in the family business, made a fortune off his IT company, and is so popular as a photojournalist he's now being offered endorsements up the wazoo."

"That's right," Gale added, still scrolling on her phone. "He might be a multi-millionaire from his own IT business, but I can't find out how much the family business is worth. That's, well, more."

Wanda was speechless. Her James? That nice guy? That rich? Was that possible?

"I assumed his room at the Grand Hotel was paid for by the people who hired him to come here. Now I wonder. It was odd but, truthfully, we were so preoccupied I didn't give it a second thought at the time. We left the Grand and walked a few houses down on the West Bluff and stayed at a beautiful cottage – although it's really a mansion – a cottage he said he'd 'arranged' to stay at for the next few days while he's still here. I figured, again, his employers gave him the place and it was arranged with the people who owned it, who weren't there."

"Ah ha," Gale went on, "they weren't there because they sold it to him the other day. I don't know what he paid, but my realtor site says it was listed for $7,500,000. Lock, stock, and barrel. Furniture, carriage, horses, driver. Probably a stocked fridge. New rolled up undies in the bedroom bureau. You name it. He got it."

"Seven and half million dollars?" Wanda almost choked. "I wonder why he didn't tell me he owned it. Wait. I know."

"Ah ha," Dawn nodded. "He was making sure you didn't want him for his money."

"I bet that happens to him all the time," Gale speculated. "He'd be stupid not to be careful about it. And he's not stupid."

A stab of fear struck at Wanda's chest. Somebody that rich – would he really want her when he could have so many other women? But then she remembered the night before and shivered with satisfaction. That had been real. Their budding romance was real. She believed that in every fiber of her being, as if they'd always been meant to be together.

"Well, you deserve somebody with some cash after what you put up with. Let's not even say the douchebag's name anymore," Dawn suggested.

"Wait a minute," Wanda said. "If his family makes yachts, does he have one here?"

"I don't know." Gale shrugged.

"We need to find out," Dawn insisted, "because I want me one nice yachtette ride before we have to head for home."

"What time is your appointment with Alexandra?" Gale suddenly wanted to know, always the one to be organized and on time.

"What? Oh! I have to go. See you later." Wanda gulped down the last of her coffee and hustled out of the there having no time now to change. Thank God she'd brushed her teeth before leaving the hotel. And there had been that shower, too. Ah, the shower ... she reminisced as she hopped on her bike and headed for the village.

As she neared Alexandra's house, however, her mind turned back to her ancestors. On the phone Alexandra had been excited to tell Wanda she'd found something, and Wanda couldn't wait to see what it might be. Had Gichi, too, like her, been in love? Had she found the love of her life? Had she been happy?

Wanda pedaled quickly to find out what new Gichi story awaited.

19

OCTOBER 25, 1830

A cry rang out from the crowd as Gichi fainted. Many a hand reached out to try to soften her fall, but none succeeded. Alexsie and Josette were the first to rush to her side and squat down to help. Alexsie pulled her shawl off her own shoulders and wadded it up to place under Gichi's head. Josette patted her fallen friend's cheek and cooed her name.

"Gichi. Gichi, dear. Wake up."

Niall McIntyre jostled his way through the crowd, having heard the name.

"Gichi? What has happened? She's fainted?" He, too, stooped down in concern.

She opened her eyes to see the man of her dreams, Niall McIntyre, bending over her. How many times had she fantasized this very thing? But not in a crowd. And not with clothes on.

"Niall?" she managed to whisper.

"Aye. 'Tis me himself. Happy to see me bonnie colleen, but not on the ground." He smiled that brilliant smile of his and Gichi instantly felt better. When she started to sit up, he took her hand to help her stand.

"Is the dear lass all right?"

The question emanated from a soft, lilting voice. A pretty, young woman with burnished copper hair appeared next to Niall. In an obviously practiced gesture, he strapped an arm across her back. She wove one arm around his waist and with the other placed a delicate hand on his swarthy chest. Gichi was struck by the interloper's natural beauty and the sprinkling of freckles across her nose. The woman's familiarity with Niall was gut-wrenchingly jarring.

Gichi didn't understand. And then she did.

Finding her voice, the voice he had helped her discover when she was seven years old, she said, "Niall, it's so good to see you again. And you must be ..." she gave the intruder her bravest attempt at a smile "... Niall's wife."

"Hello, Gichi. Yes, I'm Saoirse. I'm so happy to meet you after hearing so much about Niall's little sister. Are you okay? Your head – did you hurt it?" Saoirse lightly touched Gichi's hair.

The Irishwomen's concern, sincerity, and unpretentiousness gulled Gichi. Not to mention her beguiling loveliness. Gichi couldn't help but see why Niall had fallen in love with the witch. Gichi hated her on sight. But when the Irishwoman reached out to embrace her, Gichi found it impossible to resist.

When Saoirse let go and stood back, Gichi turned her attention to the crowd, as all eyes were on her because she'd collapsed. "I'm fine, everyone. Truly." She called out loudly. "I slipped and fell is all. But nothing broken or even bruised."

"Oh, Gichi, I'm so glad to hear it." Niall grabbed her in a big bear hug, pulled away, and nodded to the gathering reassuringly. "I must introduce you to my family," he announced to all. A boy who looked to be about seven years old ran up to him, followed by a girl about five, followed by another boy who was, Gichi estimated, three. Niall introduced each of them to the gathering as best he could while they ran around like raucous ruffians. "And there's another on the way!"

Saoirse laid a hand on her stomach, which had yet to show signs of pregnancy, grinned, and nodded. Congratulations poured over the couple.

A sweet-looking elderly woman appeared and Niall introduced his mother. All notice veered away from Gichi and she became lost in the crowd. Chief Joe joined the gathering and he and Niall and other men struck up a lively conversation. Bernard drove up with Madame sitting beside him in the buckboard. They joined the impromptu celebration of the return of the island's old friend. Niall was surprised they hadn't known he was coming, saying he'd sent a letter, but Madame assured him it had never arrived or she would have had a welcome party prepared.

Someone produced a stump for Saoirse to sit on as she was drawn into welcoming conversations. Even Alexsie and Josette seemed fascinated with her and listened in as Niall's wife described their long journey from Ireland to Mackinac Island.

Gichi, quite forgotten, stood back watching the happy and chaotic event. Alone, she thought, even in her dreams. The man of her romantic fantasies had evaporated as surely as smoke wanders up into the sky, never to return.

With a heavy heart, she turned to leave but movement back on the boat caught her eye. Two Métis oarsmen and another man transported trunks, boxes, and satchels from a second canoe onto the deck. She walked closer to watch. Finished with their task, the man handed the oarsmen money, and the Indians got back in their canoes and started out across the lake to return to the south shore. The man looked up, saw her, and walked straight toward her.

Should she run? He seemed so intent. Who was he? He stopped three feet from her. Neither of them spoke. He simply eyed her up and down. She eyes him back. And she thought she might faint again.

There stood the spitting image of Niall eight years ago. He was younger than Niall, perhaps two or three years older than she.

He graced her with what she now understood to be the dazzling McIntyre smile.

"You're Gichi. Me brother described a girl, but you are the most beautiful woman I've ever seen."

"And you, sir, are full of Irish blarney."

"Aye. That I am. I'm Liam. As you can see," he said as he held out his arms, presenting himself in all his masculine glory, "a younger, much more handsome version of me much older, much uglier brother."

She couldn't hold back a snicker. "You're quite arrogant, are you not?"

"Ah, no, I am not. I jest. But here's what you must do: you must get to know me better to decide for yourself."

"And how would you suggest I get to know you better?"

"You could accompany me tomorrow on a jaunt around this island, which I've been told you know from end to end. I'd like to get to know me new home. But first we travelers must rest from our journey." His little niece ran up and wrapped her arms around his knee. "And I promised to help with the wee ones while we get settled."

"Uncle Liam," the girl said, dropping her head back to look at him, "I seen lots of fish in that water, aye?"

"Aye, me love. Lots."

The child ran off.

Liam shrugged.

"I have a daughter. She's a month old. I doubt you want to get to know a woman who already has a child."

"Ah, so you are married then. Niall warned me of the possibility."

She considered how much to reveal. "My husband died." She didn't bother with the little detail that she'd come from the man's funeral only half an hour earlier.

"Oh, my regrets. That must be difficult."

His condolence was genuine, so she wasn't about to reveal that it wasn't difficult at all.

"I'll take you around the island tomorrow. We'll see if I still think you're arrogant by the time we're done."

"That's grand. The part about showing me around." His eyes twinkled with merriment. "As for your bairn, it only seems fair you would share yours with a penniless, wifeless, childless man like me. As for finding out if I'm as arrogant as I seem, I somehow feel certain it's nothing you can't handle."

The young couple silently faced one another for a few long moments, but Gichi didn't need any more time or any further convincing. She already knew her fate had been sealed.

20

JUNE 25, 2022

When Wanda arrived, Alexandra's elderly face crinkled jauntily as she took one look and snorted a laugh. "Rough night, huh? Sorry I scheduled this for so early in the morning. My day is booked. But I think you'll be glad to see what I found."

Alexandra poured them each a cup of coffee. Wanda figured the woman drank enough caffeine to wake the dead and was grateful for her own cup. Sitting in their usual places, Alexandra handed Wanda a copy of a letter written in elegant old-time cursive. Wanda leaned in to read it.

"It's hard to follow," she said. "This handwriting is so lovely, but I can't read it all. What's this word?"

"Gichi."

"You found Gichi? Oh, how wonderful!"

"Yes, isn't it. This is a letter written by one of the teachers at the Mission School. Apparently Gichi was a student there. An excellent one. The teacher wrote to their diocese leaders to ask for more books, especially history books, because this student had read them all. I have no idea if this request was ever granted, but the important thing is the name."

"Where on earth did you find this?"

"Online, when I looked into the history of the school." She opened her laptop as she spoke and navigated to a ready tab. "Look carefully." She slid the laptop over so Wanda could see the screen. "It says that student is Geneviève St. Croix, who the Odawa call Gichi for her full Indian name Gichigama. It was common in recording Indian names for American authorities, like Indian agents, teachers, preachers, and priests, to use names that were more familiar to them. We seldom know the name a Native used in daily life. It makes finding them difficult. But in this case, having a last name to go with Gichi led me to baptisms at Saint Anne's and, sure enough, there she is." She clicked on another tab.

The top said, "Library of Congress. The Mackinac Register, 1695-1821: Register of Baptisms and Interments." It stated that it was a transcription of the original that was handwritten and difficult to read.

Alexandra pointed to a line on the screen. "This is from 1818."

Wanda looked more closely and gasped. She read aloud. "On the same day in the same year, the undersigned missionary priest, Baptized conditionally Geneviève, three years old, a natural daughter born of J. B. St. Croix and a savage mother. The father was present. The godmother was Madame La Framboise, who declared she could not sign her name when thereunto requested. Gabriel Richard, priest."

Wanda stared at the screen, exhilarated and aghast at the same time. "Alexandra, I'm so happy to have found Gichi. But her mother – a 'savage'? How cruel."

"I know, I know. But let me tell you more about this. We may not like it today, but then Natives were often called 'savages', even in official records. That, apparently, was easier for white people than trying to figure out the tribes. I'm not saying the Natives liked it and accepted it, either. I'm only saying it was common practice. Now, 'natural daughter' means the parents weren't married in the church. Of course, because there wasn't a permanent priest, that was common, too. In fact, Gichi was probably baptized at age three because it was the first time in her life a priest was available. The fact that this J. B. was present at the baptism indicates he cared about the mother and child. I've read through many of these where the father was not present."

"Is there any way for me to do more digging into the life of this J.B.?" Wanda asked.

"Probably not, but it's worth a shot. His name is French, which means he was undoubtedly a fur trader. They often moved around and are hard to track. Most of those marriages were arranged with tribal leaders to seal trade deals. And the reality is that some of those traders had French-Canadian wives back home, wherever that might have been."

Wanda stared at the document, doing her best to keep up and take it all in. "Madame La Framboise is listed as the godmother. Her name is spelled differently here than on the information I have. In the booklet I have it's one word – Laframboise."

"That's because the French name has been Anglicized over the years, like so many things."

"The Bible has Cassandra as the daughter of Geneviève. Did you find a birth record or baptism record for her?"

"Not yet. Births weren't recorded unless a child was baptized, and then the record usually only gave the age. We have to guess birthdates from that. I'll keep looking, though. Here, dear, take back your Bible and your necklace." Alexandra took the items from their spot on her side of the table and handed them over. "We've done all we can with these for now. I made a copy of the family tree. I've put it into your family tree on ancestry.com."

"Thank you so much. This gives me a lot to work with. I'll keep researching."

"Good. Between the two of us, we might figure out more."

Wanda took the necklace out of its box and held the locket in her palm, running a finger over the smooth surface.

"Alexandra, I want to do what you do. How can I do that?"

"Really? Well, I'll be. I need help, that's for sure. I could teach you."

"Oh, will you? That would be wonderful. I need a job. A purpose. And I love this."

The elder patted her hand. "Good. We'll work together online after you go back home. The pay is decent. But right now, I need to get ready for my next client. But I don't want you to move a muscle. Stay right there. There's something you and the next person both need to know."

Wanda popped open the locket and read the inside. Alexandra had stood up and started to leave the room, but Wanda stopped her. "Did you find Niall?"

The genealogist tossed out a cockeyed grin.

A knock at the door saved her from answering the question. Instead, she answered the door.

"Hello James. Come in. We were just talking about you. Except Wanda didn't know it. My, you look beat."

James followed Alexandra into the kitchen, and he and Wanda exchanged a look that sent a sexually charged current sizzling through the room, so obvious a person would have needed to be dead and buried to miss it.

"Oh," Alexandra stated. Then she giggled. "I see. Okay then. This is the most incredibly amazing coincidence. Let's get down to brass tacks so you two can go set the world on fire."

James sat next to Wanda, producing an urge to grab him for a kiss. Instead, their knees brushed and they had to settle for that for the time being.

Alexandra got James a cup of coffee, refilled the other cups, then got down to business.

"James, you've always known your Irish ancestors started here on Mackinac Island, but you didn't have the details. And Wanda, we've discovered that your five times great-grandmother was an Odawa native here named Gichigama Geneviève St. Croix. Well, I found a connection that should be of interest to both of you."

She opened a tab on her laptop and turned it around for the two of them to read. Their heads almost touched as they bent over the screen.

"Wanda, I found your elusive Niall. And James, I found your ancestor, your five times great-grandfather, in the same person. These are baptism records from Saint Anne's for the children of Niall McIntyre and his wife Saoirse. I don't have definitive proof this is the Niall of the locket, but I'm 99 per cent sure. He was the only Niall around. But as you can see, he may have given Gichi a locket, but he was married to someone else. It's fascinating – no, downright ironic – that you two got, um, together here on the island and your ancestors knew each other here in 1822."

Wanda and James stared at the screen in tandem.

"James," Alexandra continued, "click the tab on top labeled Galway."

James clicked and once again the two of them focused on the screen.

"It's the marriage of Niall and Saoirse in 1823 in Galway," James said. "So he was here in 1822 and back in Ireland in 1823 getting married."

"And then later he and his wife were back here having their children baptized?" Wanda puzzled it together.

"Exactly." Alexandra nodded emphatically. "And we know from church records that he and several siblings were born and baptized in Galway. So he must have come here as a young man, met Gichi, gave her a locket for some reason we don't know because she was a child at the time, and then he went back to Galway, got married there, and came back here. Can you imagine? What a story!"

"I'd give anything to know the whole story," Wanda said, transfixed on the screen. "Why did Niall give a locket to a child?"

"Maybe they were friends somehow," James speculated. "A native girl and a foreigner forming a friendship for some reason we don't know."

"That we most likely will never know," Alexandra admitted. "But there's more." She cackled mischievously.

"What? Oh no, should we be afraid?" Wanda joked, sort of.

"Click the tab for 1830."

For several minutes they read off the screen then looked at Alexandra in confusion.

"Don't worry," she reassured them. "You're not blood related, only related through marriage."

Wanda looked at James and the first thought that popped into her head was that they might not be related from their ancestors' pasts, but she sure hoped they would be in the future. James seemed to be having the same thought.

Alexandra informed them that the graves of their ancestors were within walking distance at Ste. Anne's cemetery. After thanking her and paying, they went to the lovely old cemetery, stunned that the forebears they sought were right there the whole time. James had even taken pictures of her with the cemetery's stone fence as a background. It was a large place. It took them some time to find what they were looking for but there they were, the family gathered together. The headstones were eaten away and barely legible, but when Wanda finally found her five-times great-grandmother Gichi's grave with a headstone that said, "Geneviève McIntyre, beloved mother and wife, 1815-1900," she wept.

21

DECEMBER 25, 1830

The wedding took place at Ste. Anne's Church.

The bride wore a creamy white velvet gown made for her by Mother and Madame. A sheath with beaded fringe but with lace, as well, it proved a perfect combination of Odawa, Irish, and American dress. Alexsie and Josette fixed her hair in a French braid with a lovely shell comb at her crown.

When she walked down the aisle to face her groom, tears misted his eyes. "Gichi," he whispered, "you are my heart."

"And you are mine, my love."

Liam wore his Sunday clothes, a clean linen shirt and vest, along with a fine leather coat loaned to him by Chief Joe. Her groom looked as dashing as any prince she had ever fantasized in her dreams. He'd even managed to somewhat tame his unruly black hair.

They were a stunningly handsome couple, but their joy alone rendered them beautiful.

Father Mazzuchelli officiated. He'd also performed the reverent, candlelit Christmas Midnight Mass a mere fourteen hours earlier and Christmas Day Mass only five hours earlier. Therefore, the church still harbored a bevy of candles, lit for this occasion as well, and wintertime greenery that filled the space with the pleasing aroma of pine and holly.

Mother with Cassandra in her arms, Madame La Framboise, and Bernard Sterling sat in the front row on one side, while Ma McIntyre sat across the aisle alongside Niall, Saoirse, and their little ones. It appeared that most of the townsfolk had come, filling the pews to the brim with the overflow standing in the back. Even the unruly rapscallions who lived on the island were there, behaving quite properly.

A momentary realization struck as Gichi looked out to see the same faces as those in attendance at her first husband's funeral a mere two months earlier. She swept the unpleasant memory away.

She noticed that Reverend and Mrs. Ferry of the Protestant Mission Church accepted the invitation to attend, and that pleased her. After all, they had been the founders of the school Gichi attended and she felt a debt of gratitude for her education.

Later Liam would say, in his fisherman's lingo, "The church was packed to the gills."

After all, Gichi had always been a favorite of the islanders. And the McIntyres had become an integral part of the community with their fishing business taking off and their charming family easily fitting in.

Once they each said "I do" and the ceremony ended, everyone bundled up for the short walk next door to Madame's house, where a reception awaited. As the bride and groom exited the church, the sun broke out from behind feathery white clouds to beam light down upon them.

"Liam, it's a blessing on our marriage!" Gichi exclaimed.

"Surely, 'tis that."

He swept her up in his arms to carry her to the house. She laughed at his spontaneity, knowing this life with Liam McIntyre would never be boring.

Although deep snow lined the path, hundreds of footsteps had tamped it down to make walking easy. With nary a wisp of wind, the day felt like a slice of snowy white heaven.

Inside the house, everyone marveled at the feast set before them on the dining room table. Half the town, it seemed, had brought something to share. While the church had been quiet throughout the solemnity of the Nuptial Mass, the house filled with joyous laughter and cajoling and even a bit of rowdiness on the part of the children. Niall and Saoirse were full of hugs for the bride and groom, teasing that soon they would add more rambunctious children to the family.

The young couple beamed with happiness at the gathering of their families and friends and neighbors. The celebration of their love proved perfect.

"We have a surprise for you," Liam told his bride after everyone had eaten their fill.

"What? What could possibly be left?"

He grabbed her hand, led her into the front hall, helped her don her wrap, and threw on his own winter wool coat. "Everyone, come along!" he bellowed. "Gichi is going to see the surprise we have waiting for her!"

"What ..." But before she could finish he had her outside, where Bernard awaited in the buckboard.

Liam helped her up and climbed in beside her for the short ride to the center of town. The wedding guests followed on foot, the buckboard serving as Pied Piper.

Along the way they passed the small wood-slat cottage he had built for her, their potential brood, and his mother. Gichi loved looking at it as they rode by, the lace curtains given to Ma McIntyre by Madame hanging in the front windows. She had the best of all worlds – taking Cassandra with her to work with her mother during the day in Madame's kitchen, then going home to Liam and his ma, who Gichi had come to love. She had always lived with her mother, so was delighted to have yet another mother in her life.

Niall and Saoirse had a cottage next door, so Gichi and Liam's lives were already lively and full of family. Gichi found it ironic that Niall had become her big brother, albeit in-law, after all. And she marveled at how she'd gone from despising Saoirse on the day they'd met to adoring her like a sister.

As they rounded a bend, Gichi turned away from the cottages and looked ahead. She could see the surprise from two blocks away. "Liam! It's a Christmas tree!" She threw her arms around his neck and nearly toppled him over with a hug.

"Aye, me love. You told me there had never been another since Niall left, and the German man had left, too, and you had grown to love the Christmas tree. I wanted you to have another on this special day."

When they reached the tree, Bernard pulled up on the reins and Liam hopped out, then lifted her out. The others gathered around as they all stared up at the lush blue spruce tree that stood in the middle of the road, decorated with strings of berries and small tin stars. A scrim of snow swathed the spruce in a soft, diaphanous beauty.

"Thank you," Liam called out to the crowd, his melodious Irish brogue charming, his delivery dauntless, "for the many gifts you have bestowed upon my dear bride and me on this glorious Christmas Day. Secretly putting up the tree and decorating it while Gichi was at home preparing for our wedding. You would make excellent brigands sneaking about in the night." The crowd burst out in laughter. "And thank you for attending our nuptials and for the bounty you brought to the table for our reception. And, most of all, thank you for your friendship. May God bless you all!"

"Hear ye, hear ye!" someone shouted, and others joined in and applauded. Gichi clapped loudest of all, proud of this man she could now call her husband.

Chief Joe appeared at her side. "Gichi, this time I made sure a prayer was sent to the Great Spirit to thank this tree for making humans happy. It has been blessed."

"Thank you, Chief," she said, proffering a side hug. "It does indeed bring hope and happiness to those who see it."

Looking back at the tree, as her heart filled with joy over all that had transpired on this day, she suddenly became overwhelmed with a desire to use her voice to share her thoughts with the townsfolk. The little girl who'd had no voice now burst with a desire to speak.

She raised her arms to quiet the crowd. All eyes turned to her in quandary.

"Dear Ones, those of us who have spent our lives wandering this island know a secret: There lives within the soul of this mound of earth a promise to you ..." she pointed around the crowd, her voice reverberating with bold emotion and then softening "... and to me." Her dulcet voice strong again, she continued. "It is a solemn vow as binding as that between a bride and groom, the most precious Christmas gift we could receive, a promise to all who open their hearts and minds and souls when they set foot upon our island, be it for a day or for a lifetime, that their lives will be forever lifted. Their sorrows will be swept away in the wind, their hearts will be filled with the warmth of the sun, and their spirits will be renewed as surely as the waters of our great lakes flow and renew every moment of every day. Our island is a haven that offers a promise of solace in its beauty and joy in the friendship of its people. And most of all, love to all who allow it into their hearts."

She looked at Liam to gauge his reaction to her speech. Some men didn't like their wives to be outspoken. But she knew better of her Irishman. And he knew better than to try to stop her. He stood there straight and tall, a glint of pride in his eyes and his mouth arched in pleasure. She grinned at him, then turned back to the others.

"As our island has been sacred to Native Peoples for generations in the past, it shall be sacred to All Peoples for generations yet to come, now and forevermore."

She'd raised her arms in her fervor and let them fall to her side to indicate she had no more to say. The girl who'd had no voice had spoken her piece.

"Amen!" someone called out.

"Hear ye, hear ye," said another.

"Bravo!" a woman cheered.

Many of them approached the couple with more congratulations, and they mingled with each other, as well. Slowly, as the celebration began to close, they scattered, trekking through the snow to their own homes.

Eventually, only Gichi and Liam remained, with Bernard waiting for them on the buckboard.

"Bernard, go home. We'll walk," Gichi told him.

"Are you sure? Your mother told me to drive you so you wouldn't ruin your dress."

Gichi laughed. "I promise to be careful with this lovely dress. Besides, I don't know when I'd ever wear it again. This is the last wedding I ever intend to have."

The wizened old fellow nodded and drove away, the horse snorting in the brisk winter air.

Gichi stared up at the pretty tree. "This was such a thoughtful gift, my love. Thank you."

"It was nothing compared to the gift you've given me today by becoming my wife."

As they lost themselves in a heavenly kiss, a dusting of snow began to fall, sparkling flakes sheathing them in the wonder of winter on their island. They parted, looked up at the tree, gazed out at the frozen lake, and let their eyes fall back onto each other. They couldn't resist.

They kissed again.

And again.

22

DECEMBER 25, 2022

The wedding took place at James's lovely cottage, now Wanda's cottage, too, on Mackinac Island.

The bride wore a long creamy gown with a scoop neck, which Dawn insisted was perfect for accentuating her beguiling figure. Wanda did feel beautiful, in fact the most beautiful she'd ever felt in her life. It felt good.

She carried a bouquet of ivory roses. Gale fixed her hair in a French braid tucked in at the end with a rhinestone encrusted filigree brass clasp at the nape of her neck. The bride wore Gichi's brass locket from Niall in honor of both her and James's direct ancestors who had brought them to the island in the first place, as if reaching out from the past to bring them together.

When she walked into the living room, all eyes turned away from the stunning view of Lakes Huron and Michigan out the full-length windows along both sides of the fireplace and settled on her. A collective gasp rang out.

The music from the movie *Somewhere in Time*, which had become a favorite of both the bride and the groom, played softly in the background.

When she reached James's side, he swiped at a tear and whispered, "Sweetheart, you are a vision."

"And you take my breath away."

He wore an elegant black suit. She adored it that he hadn't gone with a stuffy tuxedo.

They were a stunning couple who'd found their stride in midlife, and they were elated for it.

Friends and family had helped decorate the cottage with wintertime greenery, which filled the air with the scent of pine. Candles abounded and were lit for this occasion, even though it was midafternoon. A wood fire cackled in the fireplace.

The Justice of the Peace performed the brief, simple ceremony. Afterward, everyone enjoyed a catered buffet. The small group of guests included Alexandra Ames, who'd stayed longer in the season than usual to be there. James had arranged for their families and friends to fly to the island and stay in houses he rented for them. When they left, the newlyweds would spend their honeymoon right there at the cottage. James would spend the month of January photographing Mackinac Island in the wintertime.

Once the buffet table looked like it'd been ransacked by scavengers, many of the guests and the newlyweds bundled up to walk down the bluff road to the center of town, where a brightly decorated Christmas tree stood in the middle of Main Street. It was tradition on the island to hold a Christmas bazaar every December and have a celebration for the lighting of the tree. On this Christmas Day, like so many others in the years before, the magnificent blue spruce was lit up in all its colorful splendor. Other folks and the wedding party milled around wishing each other a merry holiday, everyone in a jolly mood.

A thin veil of freshly fallen snow blanketed the scene. Gray clouds assembled above and more light snow fell upon the gathering. Suddenly, however, the clouds parted and a ray of sunshine beamed down, illuminating fat frozen flakes that continued to fall from above. It was a shower of diamonds, leaving the crowd marveling at the sight.

As they looked up at the tree, watching the sparkling glowdrops fall upon its boughs, James stood behind Wanda, wrapped his arms around her, and nestled her into his chest. She clasped his hands and turned her head to look up at him.

"James, I can feel Gichi and Niall with us today, sending their love. Can you feel them?"

He kissed her rosy cheek. "Yes, I believe I can. I believe they're happy for us."

"Yes." She looked back at the tree. "Happy for what they've done, giving us their gift of everlasting love. Let's promise that we'll pass that love on to others. Will you promise with me?"

Her beloved James rocked back and forth dreamily as he encased her in his arms. "Yes, sweetheart. I promise."

"I promise, too."

Wanda turned around so they could seal their promise with a luscious kiss.

And then another.

THE END

WOULD you like to read more from Linda Hughes?

For bonus materials about Mackinac Island and updates on the next book in this trilogy, *The Promise of Christmas Present,* which will be out in 2023, and all of Linda's books, visit her website and sign up for her newsletter. www.lindahughes.com

You are also invited to join Linda's private Facebook reader group, where you'll find special offers and a lot of fun: https://fb.me/g/ 2qd29a98o/erV2Q33W

Made in United States
North Haven, CT
16 July 2023